THE
GATEKEEPER

THE
GATEKEEPER

A NOVEL

To: Marshall

Enjoy THE GATEKEEPER!!!!

Michael A Bowling

MICHAEL A. BOWLING

Library of Congress Control Number:		2012911934
ISBN:	Hardcover	978-1-4771-3672-0
	Softcover	978-1-4771-3671-3
	Ebook	978-1-4771-3673-7

To order additional copies of this book, contact:
Xlibris Corporation
1-888-795-4274
www.Xlibris.com
Orders@Xlibris.com
116422

Contents

CHAPTER I

The Representative

LEON HARKLESS WOKE with a start to total darkness . . . *Where am I? Where was I? What day is this?* As he pondered those questions, he became aware of another presence in the room, a quiet, deliberate shuffling sound, non-threatening. Someone was moving about the room in total darkness. Normally, Leon would embrace the darkness. It had always been his ally in the past, allowing him to move though the shadows with anonymity, bringing him close to his prey without being discovered, letting him see into the brightness of a bedroom or a family room without being seen. For as long as Leon could remember, he had been in the shadows, first of his elder brothers, then of his co-workers, he had always been the grey man, everyone's acquaintance, but no one's friend. And for that reason, he had always preferred the company of children over adults. As he grew older, he made excuses to be with children, always quick to volunteer to babysit or attend birthday parties. Leon liked children. He liked everything about them. In years past, he had been content to be the voyeur, watching and fantasizing from afar. But lately, Leon had longed for and experienced more. Now, his desire was almost insatiable.

That's it! he thought. *I remember.* Elm Street, the Slater house, he had been watching Margie Slater. For the better part of a month, he had watched her, and soon he would have her and the memory of her, or would have if he hadn't woken to the present darkness.

Like always, he had parked his old van at the twenty-four-hour café, slipped out the back end of the parking lot, then crossed the vacant lot behind the old furniture factory, and ended up almost exactly behind the Slater house, where he climbed the big maple in the back and watched the comings and goings of the family. After a particularly frustrating night watching for a glimpse of Marjorie to no avail, the last thing he remembered as he stomped grudgingly back to his van was telling an old bum to f–off after he asked Leon for a cigarette. So how did he get here, and what was this feeling brewing deep in his bowels threatening to turn stool to liquid like a sudden onset of the flu? It came to him like a shooting star. You hear about them and then one day you look up and there it is, your first shooting star. Yes, it was a first. For the first time in his life, Leon was afraid. He had always made other people afraid, mothers, fathers, grandmothers, but mostly children. He liked to feed off the fear of others. He was almost embarrassed to admit it stimulated him. But this fear was not of his making and he did not like it. With all the courage he could muster, his voice cracked as he tried to demand, "Who's there?" No answer. The shuffling continued, this time the unmistakable sound of equipment being moved across the floor. "I said wh . . . who's there and what the hell is this all about?" Leon could hear his own heart beating in his chest as he looked into the darkness, willing his eyes to pierce the dark veil and expose his unseen foe.

A voice answered from the void. "This is about justice, and the rendering of it. You could say I represent justice." With that statement, a bright light shone in Leon's face almost blinding in its intensity. As his eyes focused, he realized that he was secured firmly to a chair of some kind. Visions of a dentist or doctor's chair stirred his memory, very secure, no escape. In front of him, he could see a video camera on a tripod with a man standing behind it. The man spoke. "Please state your full name and the crime that you were most recently acquitted of."

The wheels in Leon's brain slowly began to grind, *Did he say please? And acquitted?!* Leon's fear began to fade. His old confidence returned. After all, the man in front of him looked more like a state representative than a representative of justice. "F–you!" Leon spat. Instantaneous pain like nothing he had ever felt surged through Leon's body, causing his eyes to roll back in his head and his fingers to look more like claws than fingers. His whole body convulsed for what seemed like an eternity. Then, just as quickly as it started, it stopped. Relief, sweet relief. Only then did he see the two small electrodes protruding from his torso, one just below his left nipple and one in the center of his small round pot belly. Taser darts! Each one had a wire attached that ran to a controller that the man held in his hand. "You f–ing Tasered me! What the–' More pain, longer than before, ripped through his gangly body. "OK, OK! You're the boss, justice rep, what the hell ever. My name is Leon Harkless. I was recently charged with hurting a girl, but they threw it out of court because I'm innocent!"

"Wonderful! Thank you, Leon. Now we're getting somewhere. Let's make this as painless as possible, shall we? I ask the questions, you answer them truthfully, and we will try and make sense of your story. Then we can proceed from there. Understand?"

"I understand," Leon said.

"Where are your trophies?"

Leon knew instantly what he wanted, but chose to play stupid. "My little league team won the regional championships last year, but assistant coaches didn't get a trophy only the head . . . coooooaaaaches." Five thousand volts surged through his body again, not as long this time, but long enough.

"Let me clarify myself, Leon. Where are the souvenirs of your crimes?"

Behind his beady eyes, Leon's gears were turning fast now. The decision process seemed simpler and distilled. Answers came quick and easy. "Under the bed, my apartment, in the toolbox. The first tray is full tools. You'll find what you're looking for under it."

"This toolbox?" the man said as he lifted the old toolbox up on to the table.

"Yeah, that toolbox. How the hell did you get it?"

"After I picked you up, so to speak, I just swung by your apartment, used your keys to let myself in, and found it hidden ever so cleverly under your bed. Mind if I take a look?"

"Knock yourself out. You're the one running this show."

The man lifted the lid and carefully removed the top tray.

Leon mustered the courage to jeer, "What! You like to smell little girls' panties?"

The man visibly stiffened but did not look up. With something akin to reverence, he solemnly placed each item on the bed; a small blue plastic barrett, a necklace with a gold heart on it, two pairs of what were clearly young girls' underwear, and what looked to be a ballerina shoe. *Very small, too small,* the man thought as he forced himself to focus on his grim task. In the very bottom of the box, he found a small item wrapped in brown paper inside a ziplock bag. Slowly and ever so gently, he opened the bag and removed the item. Unwrapping the paper, he found what he had been looking for, a small human finger with a silver ring still on it. He carefully removed the ring and placed the finger and paper back in the bag. He held the ring up and examined it closely. It was silver with three small dolphins jumping around the entirety of the band. Inside, it said: "To Jenny, love Dad." The man stood and held the ring in front of him like a prosecuting attorney might hold a smoking gun, the case turning piece of evidence. In his mind, Leon tried to formulate a scenario in which he could explain the presence of a human finger in his toolbox. He made a quick mental list to himself, *It ain't mine! No good. I found it. Impossible. Don't know where it came from!* Leon's list evaporated.

"Tell me about Jenny, Leon."

Leon's wheels were screeching out of control now, thinking about the next dose of electricity to come his way, he involuntarily began a high-pitched pre-confession. "Oh man, that was unfortunate. That did not need to happen. It was an accident!" Leon heard his own voice echo off the block walls then fade to silence.

"Leon, it was no accident. You cut off Jenny's hands and let her bleed to death! This is where we get to the essence of what you did! And why, so we can render justice! Why, Leon, did you cut off that little girl's hands?"

Leon considered the question. He squinted into the bright light and pulled hard once more on the restraints. The last bit of courage and indignation he would ever summon welled up in Leon, and without thinking, he spat, "The bitch slapped me!" The man turned back to the camera, made what appeared to be a few minor adjustments to it, and slowly walked out of view. Leon snarled, "I guess I'm supposed to feel bad. Bullshit! I did ninety days in county for that. I paid my dues. If it hadn't been for illegal search and seizure, I might still be in jail, maybe the penitentiary. I suppose this is where you shock the shit out of me and make me piss my pants and apologize. Well, screw you, Mr. Justice Rep. I am Leon f–ing Harkless and I cower to no man."

From the shadows, the man reappeared. From his hand hung a three-foot meat axe used to quarter beef in slaughterhouses. Instantly, a small puddle of urine appeared beneath Leon's chair. The man spoke, "You have committed a crime against an innocent child, and justice cries out from the grave. We must answer." The man stepped forward and raised the huge axe. Leon's eyes bulged and his lips tried to form words, but no audible sound would come. So paralyzed with fear was he that he watched both of his hands cleaved from his body at mid-forearm without making a single noise. The man cocked his head and stared at Leon, like a puppy trying to understand his master's command. As the life blood pulsed from Leon's body and the light faded from his reptilian eyes, the man spoke, "I must say, Leon, this is a little anticlimactic, but it will do. *Justice is served*"

CHAPTER 2

Redemption

SATURDAY NIGHT AT the south side bar was always a rowdy time. Any number of different biker types, crackheads, and down-and-outs could be found there drowning their sorrows at the bar or numbing their senses in the bathroom. Anything from heroin to home-grown Michigan weed could be had, not to mention an abundance of hard liquor and even harder woman. Frequently, fights broke out over women, drugs, or the color of the patch on your back. So the bouncers tended to err in favor of safety and usually used the shock-and-awe approach to end disputes or deal with unruly patrons. Such was the case that night.

The man at the end of the bar had been there all day drinking Jack and Coke and had insulted everyone in his immediate area. Anyone who was not repelled by his odor was soon turned away by his surly attitude, including two barmaids and the owner of the establishment. The straw that broke the camel's back came when he leaned over the side of the bar and expelled a fifth of Jack Daniels and a bag of barbecue potato chips that had been percolating in his gullet all day. One look from the owner, and Eclipse, the Saturday night bouncer, made his way to the drunk. John Reetz heard the big boots coming his way and realized why they called him Eclipse as the big man towered over him and blocked what little light emanated from the ceiling. Without looking up, Reetz said, "Hey, Dummy, move your head. I can't see where I'm puking here." A meaty hand came down hard, hitting John right between the shoulder blades and driving him straight to the floor, smashing his face in his own bile. The big man unceremoniously grabbed him by his collar and dragged him down the narrow hallway that led to the back alley. Ignoring John's numerous insults, he dragged him straight out the back door and tossed him on the pavement.

"You stink, you look like shit, and you puked in the bar. Three strikes, you're out."

With every ounce of strength John could muster, he slowly pulled himself vertical. "Is that so?" he slurred with crossed eyes. "Well, the two of you are fat, you smell like Old Spice, and you're so ugly you make me wanna puke some more."

The man stared back at him for a moment with a calm demeanor. Without warning, the big head slammed forward, butting John right where his forehead touched his hairline. And the night ended for John Reetz like it had many nights before over the last two years since his life began to crumble.

Cadillac Man

The late model Cadillac slowed for the road block. An officer came up to the car's window. "I'm sorry, sir, but we have an Amber alert state-wide, a missing boy from Lincoln. We are checking all suspicious vehicles. They say the first twenty-four hours are the most critical."

"So I've heard," the man said. "You're welcome to do your job, Officer. All I have is a small suitcase and some technical manuals. I have a sales call to make in Des Moines later this afternoon."

The officer shrugged his shoulders and waved him on. "That won't be necessary. Have a nice day, and good luck with your sales call. Make a million." As the Cadillac drove away, the officer thought to himself, *Loser! Another salesman bugging the hell out of people trying to sell them shit they don't need. I'm glad I've got a real job. I help people. I protect the public.* When the next car pulled up, an old rusty Fairlane, his mental caution lights began to flash. The driver, a slightly built man in his thirties with greasy thinning hair, asked what the problem was. The officer took two steps back, and without answering the man's question, said, "Put the car in park and step out of the vehicle." He let the man see him lay his hand on his revolver. "Open the trunk now!" The officer demanded. The scared driver fumbled with his keys, trying desperately to comply. Visions of a scared young boy sitting up from the trunk flirted with the officer's imagination. But the trunk was empty. And he would not be a hero that day. He reluctantly sent the greasy man on his way. He was sure the man was guilty of something. Rarely did his cop instincts fail him. A mile down the road, in the trunk of the Cadillac, a young boy whimpered.

John rubbed the goose egg on his forehead as he stumbled up the stairs of his modest ranch house at the end Pearl Street. He had moved there to Tecumseh, Michigan fifteen years ago and taken a job at the Ford plant. He worked hard every day and loved it, got a company discount on his new 250 Super Duty pickup and had sprung for the mandatory Triton bass boat. Sure they both had books, but he was receiving the green medicine from Dr Ford. And he could make the payment easy. Ten years ago, they had their first child, a girl. He had always wanted a boy, but when his little girl looked up at him with her big blue eyes, he fell hard. She was a daddy's girl. Now it was all gone, his wife and daughter, his boat and truck. By the looks of the foreclosure notice on the front door, the house was next in line. How had he come to this place? The rising sun warmed his back as he fumbled with his key in the door. As he pushed it open, he had visions of his daughter and wife running to greet him, his lunch box in hand, his little Jack Russell, Mr. Beasley, behind them doing backflips like John had been gone for ten years instead of ten hours. He paused, slipping into neutral like he always did when those memories came. Relishing the moment, willing it to stay, but it always slipped away. And the reality of his circumstances came flooding back. The things he wanted to remember he could not. The things he needed to forget buzzed inside his head like a pesky fly. He passed through the kitchen littered with fast-food wrappers and empty alcohol containers of all sorts. As he made his way to the living room, another memory sprung at him from the corner.

Their last Christmas tree stood there at a slight angle, boughs hanging low in surrender, like it had given up on the concept of merriness. It had stood there for two years untouched. Their last Christmas had been wonderful. Christmas was always white in Michigan. They had played in the snow, enjoyed friends and family, and exchanged gifts to each other. He had gotten a sweater, a flashlight, and a pocketknife. In return, he had given his wife a blender, a bread-maker, and some hot curlers. For his daughter, he went all out, a new sled, a set of roller blades she could use when warm weather came, and a beautiful white fluffy coat made of synthetic fur from some new-age polyester creature. After all the presents were opened, his daughter jumped on his lap and hugged his neck. She put her hands on both sides of his face and pulled it close until their noses touched. Looking into his eyes without blinking, she declared, "You're the best daddy ever!" Only then did he reach into his pocket and retrieve a small blue box.

He held it up to her like a proud student offering the choicest apple to his favorite teacher. She stared at it for only a moment, then snatched it up with glee. "More?" she said. "You saved the best for last!" Slowly, she opened the velvet box. Tied to a little blue cushion with a blue ribbon was a silver ring with little dolphins jumping around the band. *Dolphins, the most beautiful creatures God ever made!* she thought. She untied the ribbon and removed the ring. Inscribed on the inside were the words: "To Jenny, love Dad." As long as John lived, he would always remember the look on his daughter's face. She was incredulous. Like a child opening a box and finding a puppy or a kitten, she could barely articulate words. "Dadolphins! Ohdadolphins! Ohdaddankyousomuch!" That pesky fly buzzed him back to the moment and brought with it bad memories, horrible memories. The ring was gone, Jenny was dead, his wife had left without saying a word. As with most couples of child abduction and murder, their union could not stand the test. She had not been mad. She just packed one bag and left for New Hampshire to see her mother. She had not called or written. He had quit his job and crawled into a bottle for two years. Now his bank account was empty, and the cold house was a shell filled with bad memories, not the warm home it had once been. His heart was not even a heart any more. It was a broken piece of flesh trying not to beat, thumping along like an old engine that kept running no matter how bad you neglected its maintenance. It was time!

John went to the kitchen cupboard and reached high on to the top shelf. He momentarily panicked as he felt around, like in the airport when you feel for your plane tickets in one pocket, momentarily panic, then find them in the other. He reached further and finally felt its smooth cool steel, his ticket out of the living hell. He pulled the gun down and checked the chamber. Like always, it was loaded. With the gun hanging at his side, John walked up the stairs, he turned left, and walked down to the last door on the left, Jenny's room. He opened the door and made his way to the bed. He lay on his back eyes closed for a long time, trying to conjure up good memories. But all he could see were autopsy photos of his baby lying there with no hands. He had seen those photos so many times he could not remember what her hands looked like, like when you haven't seen someone for a long time and you try to conjure up memories of their face, memories that just won't come. He tried to remember how her hands felt when she pulled his face close at Christmas. *Jenny! Oh Jenny! How could some monster do that to my Jenny?* He prayed, "God, I don't know if you're real, I don't know if you answer prayers, but I know that Jenny is in heaven and I want to be there with her. I have never asked you for anything, God, but I want to make this one request. The Bible says something about an eye for an eye, and a tooth for a tooth. Please, God, let the man who took Jenny from me pay for his crimes. If you will do this for me, I will stand with the angels and sing praises to you forever." Without opening his eyes, he brought the gun up and put it in his mouth. With both thumbs, he cocked the trigger. Slowly, he began to squeeze. The doorbell rang. He opened his eyes. Staring down at him from a poster on the ceiling was a smiling dolphin standing on his tail in the surf. Again the doorbell. John looked at the dolphin, *What are you smiling about? You look like you know something I don't!* Again the doorbell. It reminded John of times when he was making love to his wife and the doorbell or the phone rang. His wife would invariably say, "Let it ring, tiger." But John's curiosity would always get the better of him, and he would dive out of bed promising a prompt return. And so, he laid the gun on the bed and made his way to the stairs. Again the doorbell. He took the stairs two at a time and made it to the kitchen just as a motor started. He opened the door and stepped on to the porch as a delivery truck left the drive. He watched it disappear, then turned back to the house. As he did, he caught a glimpse of something on the porch. A small package. He picked it up and would have tossed it in the bushes if he had not read the return address: 4-justice. *Justice. What a concept!* he thought. The man that killed his baby girl was running free right now as he was about to kill himself. They had found the murder weapon with his daughter's blood on it in his car. But sloppy police work had made that case-clinching piece of evidence inadmissible in court. The jurors never were told and could not be told because the evidence was obtained without a search warrant. *Justice!* He carried the package in the house and sat on the couch. He opened it up and dumped the contents on the coffee table, a DVD and a small item wrapped in a piece of notepaper. He unwrapped the paper and could not believe his eyes. Jenny's ring inscription and all. It had never been found, neither had her hands. Her little body had been found dumped in the open along Interstate 96, just west of Detroit. He picked up the piece of paper it was wrapped in. Written with a felt marker was: "*For your eyes only.*" He picked up the DVD and walked to the TV. He turned it on and placed the DVD in the DVD player. As it whirred, he considered his options: He could go upstairs and finish what he started or he could hit play and see who knows what, the mutilation of his baby girl. Either option would kill him. Without thinking, he hit the play button. To his absolute amazement, the image of Leon Harkless, his child's murderer, appeared, strapped to a chair, being interrogated by someone off-screen. John watched the scene unfolding before him with morbid fascination, the final flash of cold steel, like the last act of a Shakespearian play. John Reetz watched the DVD in its entirety nine times. He stood up, stripped off the clothes he had been wearing for a week, and walked naked up the stairs. He went first to the bathroom sink and picked up a new razor. Slowly, he began to shave his face, watching it transform in the mirror. His blank eyes began to absorb the light that suddenly seemed to fill the room. A smile tugged at the corner of his mouth as he said, "Thank you, Lord!" He stepped into the shower and began to sing the only hymn he knew, *Praise God from Whom All Blessings Flow* . . .

CHAPTER 3

Justice

DARIUS WILLIAMS SCRAPED a pie-plate-sized hole in the light frost on the windshield of his beat-up Ford Escort . . . He jumped in quickly, fired the engine, and made his way down the side street leading to the interstate. He looked at his watch, 4:00 a.m. He would have to hurry to make it to work on time, especially looking through this small clearing in the windshield. Too bad his right wiper was the only one functioning . . . He enjoyed his job at the Detroit Metro Airport loading luggage . . . especially driving the luggage tram around the tarmac with his fluorescent orange vest . . . *Not just anyone could do his job,* he thought as he brought the old Escort up to a speed he felt comfortable with on the slippery road. He was thankful that there was only light traffic heading east to the airport. *Prolly cheap white folk who bought early departure tickets to save twenty bucks.* Darius wiped the window with an old shop towel and strained to see the road through his small portal of visibility. He leaned forward over the steering wheel to get a clearer look at the road, almost touching his nose to the windshield. The fog created by the melting frost was starting to lift, revealing vast fields of winter wheat starting to turn green in the warming March soil. Darius glanced to the right side of the road and involuntarily hit the brakes, putting the car into a spin. He stopped, facing the other direction on the berm at the side of the road. Had he seen what he thought he'd seen? He eased the car down the road, being careful to stay out of oncoming traffic . . . As the object of his interest came into the view . . . his mind flashed back to his old neighborhood in Detroit. South Livernois Avenue was as bad a neighborhood as you could find, and he had seen this picture many times before . . . with one exception. The dead body hanging on the interstate fence facing the highway had no hands, just two stumps raised to the heavens . . . The man's eyes were wide open and full of question . . . a look Darius had seen many times before on the faces of people shot in the street, a look that said, "I can't believe this happened to me!" Darius pulled out his cell phone . . . His whole body shuddered as he dialed 911.

Detective Jamie Larson hung up the phone . . . State police had a stiff out on Route 96. Apparently, it was a perp he had locked up a couple of years ago. Not much good came across his desk those days, so any time a serial child abuser was taken out of circulation, it was a good thing, no matter how it happened. He hollered at Kate, "Let's roll, girl. This one might get interesting." . . . He and Kate had been partners since she had gotten out of the academy. At first, he had hated the thought of woman partner and was absolutely ready to draw a line in the sand with his sergeant . . . until she walked into his office four years ago . . . Kate Wagner was beautiful . . . but the most attractive thing about Kate was that she didn't see what all the fuss was about . . . She really didn't see herself as good looking and hated the unwanted advances of men as much as she hated pedophiles.

Many times, Jamie had been eating lunch with her when some well-meaning guy came up to the table with a lame line about hot lady cops, asking if he could be handcuffed. Once, she had actually stood up, grabbed the guy's left wrist, and bent it at an unnatural angle. When the guy spun around to relieve the pressure, she slapped the cuffs on him and took him to the car. She returned to the table, finished her lunch like nothing had happened, and after lunch, she went to the rear passenger side of the car and let him out. She turned him around, whispered something in his ear, and took off the cuffs. The guy stumbled as he tried to go around Kate to get to his car. After the tension cleared, Jamie asked her, "What did you whisper in his ear?"

"I told him he probably couldn't handle it!"

Handle what? Jamie thought as he brought the unmarked up to speed. He considered asking her . . . then thought better of it. Kate was Kate, and he was glad she was his partner, not his love interest.

They arrived at the scene about 10:00 a.m. The crime scene team had created a makeshift curtain to block the spectacle from the general public, who could always be counted on to cause a chain reaction pile-up over the simplest deviance in their daily commute. Behind the curtain, he was shocked to find the body of Leon Harkless draped over a fence, his hands cut off . . . He was almost ashamed to admit the sight lifted his spirits . . . Only a month ago, he had testified for the prosecution in his trial . . . for the murder of Jenny Reetz . . . But an overzealous street cop had demanded that Leon open his trunk after a vehicle description matching that of Leon's had come across his radio as possibly being involved in a child abduction. The well-meaning officer was hoping to find a live little girl in the trunk, but a bloody meat cleaver wrapped in a plastic bag was all he found . . . A week later, the little girl's body was found in a ditch along this very highway not too far from this exact spot! Kate stood, notebook in hand, watching Jamie, deferring the moment to him. After working with him for four years, she found that an untimely question could muddy up his thought process like an unwanted heckler at press conference. "Get a time of death, Kate, to the hour. Then get an address for the father. This looks like payback to me. We'll go in low profile and casually ask him if he's heard the news, get his alibi for the last twenty-four hours or so. Watch his reaction. This should be a slam dunk! I mean, who would want him dead more than the father right?"

A CSI tech came up to them. "Hey, you guys might want to take a look at this."

They had removed Leon's body from the fence and placed it in a body bag. They opened the bag, revealing the chest. Carved deeply into the flesh was the roman numeral "IV" and the word "justice." Jamie looked at Kate. "Did I tell you this might get interesting?" Kate looked at him for a moment with a questioning gaze. "What?" Jamie asked.

She hesitated for a moment, then asked, "Are we gonna go hard on this or easy? This dirtbag had it coming. You know he did"

Jamie looked at her for a moment. "If someone killed you, I'd go hard after him. And you're way freaky!"

Kate laughed. "OK," she said, "I just wanted to know where your head was at. Hard it is, Detective Larson."

Kate got back from the morgue shortly after lunch. Jamie was just finishing up some Chinese takeout that smelled way too much like raw eggs and fish. She almost turned right around and walked out of his office but couldn't think of a valid reason for a hasty departure. So she took a deep breath through her mouth and strolled in like everything was golden. "So how'd it go?" Jamie asked. "You get a time of death?"

She tried to answer and avoid looking at the remnants of his lunch in unison. The sum result was a good imitation of a distressed Dustin Hoffman in *Rain Man.* Jamie immediately picked up on her discomfort and with a plastic fork, offered her a wilted piece of shrimp. "Hungry?" he said with a smile.

"No, I'm not hungry, you ass, and if I was hungry, I wouldn't eat that on a bad day!" His cocky attitude was enough to quell her sensitive stomach and steel her nerves. "Coroner says he can't give us a definitive time of death because the body was kept refrigerated or left in cold storage until it froze. Could be two days, could be two weeks. Cause of death? Sudden violent hand removed, he bled to death."

Jamie picked up a file from his cluttered desk and tossed it to Kate. "That girl he killed was dumped half a mile from where his body was recovered. I say we go pat the old man on the back, thank him for taking out the garbage, and put the cuffs on him. Right?! I mean, no one else has a motive."

Kate thought for a moment. "I don't know about that. You would have liked to put a bullet in his head, and so would I."

Jamie nodded. "Yeah, but we didn't, and we wouldn't, because we have too much to lose. Dad, on the other hand, . . ."

Kate picked up the car keys from his desk. "Let's do this, cowboy. You got a set of cuffs on you?"

"Don't start that cowboy shit again. A guy buys a pair of boots and all the sudden, he's a cowboy. High heels don't make you a hooker, do they?"

"Depends on the color and the height of the heel," Kate countered.

He smiled and opened the door ". . . after you, pard."

Cadillac Man

"Welcome to Michigan," the sign said. "It's good to be back," the man replied out loud as he pulled off the interstate and took Route 131 north to White Pigeon. He turned right on Route 12 and headed east with no particular location in mind. That part of Michigan was covered with swamps and patches of second-growth timber and hardwoods, any one of which would serve his purpose. He waited until there were no cars behind him or oncoming and pulled on to a gravel two lane not much more than a horse path. It was Amish country. People minded their own business there. If they saw the late model Cadillac parked next to the woods, they would likely think it was a city slicker trying to find the elusive Morel mushrooms so common in the spring.

He turned on to a dirt trail that wound back to a thicket and disappeared around the corner of a stand of hardwoods. The trail showed no signs of use, and the nearest house was two miles away. As he rounded the stand of oaks, he could not believe his luck. An old sugar shack stood proudly at the back, long forgotten and neglected, built of native timber, unwilling to yield and collapse, waiting for someone to build a fire and render the water-maple mix into sweet syrup again. He pulled the car around behind the shack and turned off the engine. It was midday, and the red squirrels and tree frogs seemed to be proclaiming the arrival of spring, barking and croaking incisively, like they were glad to hear their own voices after the long dormant Michigan winter. He got out and went to the shack. He pulled the door. It failed to open. Rusty hinges or swelled jamb, he couldn't tell which. It was like the old shack was protesting, unwilling to be used for other than its intended purpose. He cursed and pulled harder on the door; it groaned and opened. He stepped inside. A great square basin sat horizontally at one end with a drain in the centre. A wooden bunk lined one wall apparently to accommodate the farmer who would often spend all night tending the fire under the rendering tank. Various chairs and other utensils cluttered the room. *This is too good to be true,* he thought to himself as he lit a cigarette to calm his nerves. He went to the car and opened the trunk. Panic momentarily gripped him when the boy failed to move. He should have given him some water on the long trip east. Slowly, the boy began to move. He turned, hoping to see a familiar face. The face he saw was contorted with lust and cruel intent. He closed his eyes and prayed the prayer of the innocent.

When they arrived at the Reetz home, the outside looked in poor condition. The winter snow was receding, leaving a season's worth of sticks, twigs, candy wrappers, bottle caps, and cigarette butts littering the front lawn. It looked like the yard of a senile old man who had given up the dream of having the greenest lawn on the block. Kate knocked. A man answered the door with a smile. "Hi," he said, "can I help you?"

"John Reetz? I'm detective Kate Wagner, this is my partner Detective Larson. We are investigating a homicide. May we come in?"

"Sure, no problem."

Inside, the house seemed to be going through a renovation or a major clean-up of some kind. The smell of Lysol hung heavy in the air, and a variety of cleaning agents sat about the kitchen.

"Cleaning up?" Jamie asked with a caught-you-red-handed ring.

"As a matter a fact, I am," John said with an easy smile. "My wife is coming home tomorrow, and I want the place to feel like home when she gets here. I haven't seen her in six months."

Jamie glanced at Kate, a subtle raise of his eyebrow told her what she needed to know. He was asking her if she wanted to be the good cop or the bad cop. She opted for the latter, pulled out an autopsy photo, and handed it to John, carefully watching his face. He couldn't have looked more pleased if you had handed him a winning lottery ticket.

"That's a shame," he said, "hate it when that happens."

Jamie and Kate looked at each other. "When what happens?" Jamie asked.

"When you get your hands cut off, it must be very painful. I can only imagine what my Jenny went through." At the mention of his daughter's name, John seemed to sober a little. "Listen! You can't possibly expect me to feel bad? He killed my daughter. What do you want me to say?"

"Start by telling us when and where you killed him," Kate said.

John momentarily looked confused, and then his brow knit with concern. "You guys think I killed him? Don't get me wrong. It's been my consuming fantasy for two years. There's only one problem. I'm not a killer. I don't even own a gun. I only heard last month that he was finally released after the DA dropped the case against him."

"So you knew he was released?" Jamie asked.

"Yes!"

"You're also aware that the sexual offender registration program listed his address online the fifteenth of last month?"

"I don't have a computer right now. I wouldn't know about that," John said, his voice starting to hint of the fear invading his system.

Kate spoke. "John let me spell it out for you. A forensic team is on their way here as we speak," she lied. "They are going to turn this house upside down. Probably going find DNA evidence in the bathroom tub or sink. Most likely, they will match fibers from your living room rug to those on Leon's body. No matter what they find, you are leaving here today in cuffs. And your wife is going to come home tomorrow and find you in county lock-up charged with the murder of Leon Harkless. Nothing you can say or do is going to change those facts."

"Really!" he said. He slowly got up and walked toward the living room. Jamie inconspicuously unsnapped the clasp of his service revolver while following him. Kate watched the man with a wariness that years of police work had honed to a fine edge. He seemed to be contemplating something. She was sure he was going to bolt! He turned back toward them as he reached for his pocket. In one motion, they both drew their revolvers. John stopped. His hand buried deep in his pocket. "Sorry," he said. "I'd like to show you something?" Slowly, he pulled the ring out of his pocket and handed it to Jamie. He walked to the DVD player and hit "play." "I wasn't going to show you this, but I don't feel like going to jail today."

CHAPTER 4

The Beginning

DOWNTOWN ANN ARBOR had recently gone through a major renovation, making parts of the downtown area look like Chicago or New York City . . . lots of glass and shiny metal fascia . . . Modern artwork adorned the street corners, and parking lots were replaced by sleek parking garages. The Reynolds & Reynolds Financial Consulting building was the showpiece of the south-east corner of the city, standing as a monument to success and prosperity in the downtown area. Inside, brokers worked feverishly to expand their clients' financial holdings. On the fourth floor, Vice President Libby Reynolds was enjoying her morning cappuccino as she went over the spreadsheet of one of their larger clients, a polymer resin manufacturer whose headquarters was based in Ann Arbor. Reynolds & Reynolds had been solely responsible for tripling Progressive Polymer's liquid assets in the last year alone. The commission to Reynolds & Reynolds would exceed $350,000, a tidy sum even by company standards. Libby had risen to the top of the company hierarchy because: number one, she was highly qualified, a graduate with honors from Harvard University Business School and number two, her father was Aaron Reynolds, founder of Reynolds & Reynolds Financial.

Libby smiled as a funny thought struck her. What if she had not kept her maiden name? What would they have called the company then, Reynolds and Lombardo? It didn't exactly roll off the tongue. Raymond was Italian and proud of his name, but her father had refused to change the name of the company, and she had not argued. So she had kept her maiden name and simply added Lombardo like she was a famous Hollywood starlet. The important thing was that Raymond was a good husband and a great father to their son, Raymond Jr. The intercom buzzed and brought her back to the present.

"Is there anything I can get you, Miss Reynolds?"

"No, Mary, I'm fine, thank you. How are the kids and Dan?" Libby asked.

"Everyone is fine, Miss Reynolds. We are so excited. We close on the new house next week. We will officially be country folks!"

"Nice," Libby said, "if I need anything, I'll let you know, Mary."

Mary, like everyone in the company, seemed to be happy and prosperous. From her father, Aaron Reynolds Sr., to the lowest janitor, Dad's profit sharing plan had worked flawlessly in creating wealth for each and every employee. And every one of their clients had seen substantial gains for the last two years. Now the company was on cruise control. Her father rarely even showed up most days. She handled most of his affairs and kept him abreast of the daily operations of the company via email.

It was all in stark contrast to the bad times that began fourteen years earlier . . . the day her little brother was found dead, decapitated, his body discarded in a swamp south of Ann Arbor. It was almost like a huge dark cloud descended on her family, like one of the sudden violent storms that would sometimes hit mid-Michigan, uprooting trees and leveling buildings, changing the landscape forever. Hunters had come across the body while hunting in south Lenawee County. He had been missing for almost two weeks when the body was found. He was only nine years old. Mom and Dad would never say he was an accident, but used words like "surprise" and "gift" when speaking about her younger brother. A massive search was mounted hours after he went missing and continued until the day his body was found. Then the search for her brother's killer took on a life of its own. Dad sold his half of a modestly successful construction company to his partner for $275,000 and put up a $250,000 reward for the arrest and apprehension of the killer. Thousands of tips came in and thousands of man hours were logged, to no avail. FBI profilers were convinced that the killer had left the area or been imprisoned, that he had acted alone, and was extremely intelligent, not likely to share the knowledge of his crime with a confidant. Long story short, the case went cold . . .

Four years later, her mother contracted breast cancer and after a routine mastectomy, had simply given up. She said goodbye to her and her father, looked apologetically into their eyes, and faded away like someone might apologize for leaving a graduation party early and slip quietly out the back door. The landscape that was her life changed forever the day her little brother died. Libby had gone off to college, and her father had gone home and locked himself in the house for five long years. He wouldn't answer the phone for anyone but her or the police department, who she prompted to call every so often and assure her father they were still on the case. Mom's life insurance policy settlement had allowed him to live moderately without working and pay for her college bills, for which she was extremely grateful. The one positive thing that happened through all those years was when her father, before his self-imposed isolation started, on the recommendation of a family friend had taken the 275,000 he had gotten for selling his company and invested it in a fledgling company called Google. The stock that he purchased for $17 a share traded eight years later for over $550 a share, making Aaron Reynolds one of the richest men in the United States. Then one day, for no apparent reason whatsoever, he had gotten out of bed, shaved, showered, and had come back to the land of the living. Like Lazarus waking from the dead, he just seemed to snap out of it. And like the biblical story, friends, family, and community rejoiced at the resurrection of Aaron Reynolds.

It seemed everyone wanted a piece of him . . . Dateline, 20/20, *Forbes* magazine . . . If they weren't inquiring about the abduction of his son; they wanted to know how he predicted the rise of Google. And her father was gracious to everyone. No matter how busy he was, he would make time for any person trying to help the cause of missing and exploited children. He was a tireless crusader for children's rights. In his spare time, he started Reynolds & Reynolds Financial and put Libby at the reigns. The resurrection of her father was truly amazing to behold. He was the same loving, confident, caring person he had always been before her brother died. And to the outside casual observer, he had not changed, but Libby had noticed a very subtle change in her father. He seemed to be more decisive and less tolerant. He was quick to make important decisions and swift to meet out judgment. It was almost like the future was written and he was just reading the script, making all the right decisions on time without regrets. Yes, that was the essence of Aaron Reynolds. He hated regrets. He would rather try and fail than regret not having tried. She would put it on his memorial some day. It would say: "Aaron Reynolds, a *man without regret*"

Aaron Reynolds jumped in his truck and made his way down the long drive. He turned on to the stone road that led down to the lower pasture. He had chosen this old farm because of its remote location and low profile, no scenic vistas of his home from the road. Matter of fact, unless you were looking for Aaron Reynolds, you would not even be on the road. It dead-ended into his driveway. He had spent a couple of years making it livable, then installing security cameras about the property. He had cut a path through the thorn apple thicket in the rear that led to a logging trail that wound through the hard woods and opened up into a pasture three-quarters of a mile away. It was an escape route of sorts. In a matter of five minutes, he could be on Squaw Field Road a mere ten minutes from the interstate. His final and proudest accomplishment was the chamber, a twenty-four by-thirty-foot soundproof concrete bunker of sorts. He had paid a premium to have an out-of-state contractor dig the hole, pour the concrete walls and ceiling, and be gone in seventy-two hours. But the end result was just what he had envisioned in his mind. He set the poles and rafters for a modest pole barn with the help of some local hippies who never once noticed the twenty-four-by-twenty-four-inch access hole leading to the chamber. He had covered it with a piece of plywood and set five bags of mortar on it, enough to discourage any would-be snoop.

He purchased a video camera, a tripod, and a police scanner from a local retailer and outfitted the chamber with the proper lighting and creature comforts. It had a single drain in the middle of the floor, a sink, toilet, and shower to clean up when necessary. An old wooden restraint chair he had bought online completed the furnishings. All his years of planning had become reality, and it was satisfying to behold.

Aaron turned his truck on to the drive that led to the old pasture he had converted to a shooting range, his hand rested easily on his nickel-plated desert eagle. It was a beautiful piece of Israeli technology designed for Israeli soldiers. It had quickly become a sought-after weapon worldwide, known for its extreme accuracy and intimidating presence. Looking into the barrel of a forty-caliber desert eagle was a life-changing experience. After all, the goal was not to shoot it; it was only a means of control. Aaron did not want to shoot the men he sought. He only wanted to render justice in the same fit and fashion as they had dealt with their young victims. What was the old saying? What goes around, comes around. He had always dreamt of facing the man who had decapitated his son some day, but that dream would never be a reality. It had been fourteen years. He was probably dead or in prison. The best he could hope for was to help bring justice to the families of other murdered children, an idea that had snapped him out of his funk six years ago and had only come to fruition in the last month.

After carefully examining the case of Jenny Reetz and thoroughly researching the criminal history of Leon Harkless, Aaron had determined that Leon would be the first to visit the chamber. It had been quite simple. Aaron had followed him for a week, established a pattern, waited for him to return from his last reconnaissance mission, posed as a bum to get close and hit him with the Taser. While he was down gasping for air, he had given him a large dose of oral sedative and duct-taped his mouth, hands, and feet. He threw him in the back of the truck and closed the hatch on the cab. Without incident, he had made his way to Leon's apartment, then on to the farm. Six years of planning, strategizing, training with various weapons, restraints, and immobilizing agents had served him well on his first foray. He was ready to *unleash hell*... in a good way! IV-Justice.

CHAPTER 5

Under Pressure

AARON REYNOLDS PICKED up the *Ann Arbor Times* and began to read. Edward Hogreve would be released from the Coldwater Correctional Facility that day after serving only six years for the murder of fifteen-year-old Daniel Adkins. In a plea bargain arranged with District Attorney Mark Goldsmith, Hogreve agreed to lead detectives to the body of Daniel Adkins in exchange for a manslaughter plea. A state-implemented early release program allowed Hogreve to be released with half time served, sparking a firestorm of outrage among child activist groups. According to court records, Hogreve, a laid-off lumber mill worker, offered two young teens a ride near their Ann Arbor suburb. After the teens refused his offer, he pulled a semi-automatic pistol and forced them into his car. He then drove them to the Lost Nations State Wildlife Area in southern Hillsdale County. After forcing the two youths from his car, he marched them into the woods, where he killed Daniel Adkins with multiple blows from a camp shovel to his head and face. He then took the young girl, whose name remains undisclosed at this time, to his home in rural Ann Arbor, where he raped and tortured her for two days before she escaped after a drunken Hogreve fell asleep. He was arrested without incident an hour later, still asleep, unaware that his captive had escaped. Prosecutors said the manslaughter deal was hammered out after subsequent attempts to find the body of Daniel Adkins proved unsuccessful.

A dark shadow crossed Aaron Reynolds face as he closed the paper and opened his laptop to Google the name Edward Hogreve. After locating an address and researching his criminal history, he closed the laptop and went out to the workshed. After a little effort, he found what he was looking for, a long-billed spade used for digging narrow trenches. He picked it up and felt the weight of it. He swung it through the air a few times, nice easy strokes, like when he used to hit pop fly balls to Aaron Jr to fine tune his Little League catching skills. He laid it on his shoulder and walked confidently to the chamber like a home-run hitter walking the bases after a grand slam.

The young girl sat in the corner of the rundown trailer. She was bound and her mouth was gagged. She was having a hard time getting enough air through her nose. She had cried for so long that mucus had built up in her nostrils and was seriously restricting the passage of air. The man noticed her distress. With blank hard eyes, he stared at her; he did not care if she died. He just didn't want her to die too soon. He walked over and removed a razor-sharp hunting knife from a sheath on his side. He held it in front of her face and let the blade catch the light. Her shaking stopped, and her eyes seemed to focus. "That's right! I've got your attention now. I'm going to take off your gag so you can breathe. If you scream, I'll cut your tongue out. Then I won't have to worry about you making noise, will I?" He slid the knife between the cloth gag and the skin of her cheek and slowly pulled. The gag fell away. The girl remained silent. She stared at him wide-eyed and motionless, wanting desperately to look away but afraid of what she might not see coming. He smiled, "Yur purty. It's been six years since I've been with a purty gurl"

The girl did not acknowledge the man but rather retreated back into her mind, creating a buffer between the two of them. She had stayed the night with a friend and had started walking for home in the morning, just a half mile away. The man had pulled up and offered her a ride. He had a genuine smile and looked harmless enough, so she hopped in. She thanked him for the ride, and they proceeded down the road to her house. As the car approached her house, she could see her father mowing the lawn. He was coming toward the road on their old wheel-horse mower. Just before she made eye contact with him, he completed his lap with the mower and turned back away from the road. The driver of the car seemed to hesitate, slow down, then he resumed speed and drove right past her driveway. She watched her father happily bouncing away on the mower and realized she had made a terrible mistake.

The man smacked her face. "Hey, girly, focus. I'm gonna need to have your full attention soon . . . Don't space out on me, k? I have a few things to do, and then me and you are going to get to know each other real good." The man went to the fridge and got another beer. *Cold beer and purty gurls . . . don't get much better 'n this,* he thought. He had dreamed of this night since he went to the penitentiary . . . He'd even made a list of equipment he would need to make or buy. He hated to kill this one . . . *She was so purty.* If he'd been a little smarter, he could have built a box or a kennel of some kind and kept her for a few days. But he wasn't smart and he knew it. He liked to think of himself as a crocodile . . . They ain't real smart; they just sneak up on shit and eat it, and they don't feel bad afterwards. One thing for sure; she wasn't going to sneak off when he wasn't looking and get the police involved. He would be exhausted when the night was over, but he'd let the air out of her before he went nappin'. He went to the back room of the trailer and made a quick inventory of things he would need. This had to be done right. He had dreamed of this night for six years. On the wall was a checklist with two dozen things he wanted to make happen that night. He felt a stirring in his loins . . . too bad his old cellmate, Bennie, couldn't be here. Half the ideas on the list were his. Bennie was real smart . . . *He woulda built a box for sure.* But Bennie hadn't made parole on the early release program. They said he was too dangerous. Ed was almost offended that they didn't think he was too dangerous . . . but he played along and said all the right things and even went to prison chapel every Sunday. After his release, the only place he could get a job was at a nursing home. Everybody else was scared by his record. Maybe the nursing home people figured that since he wasn't nice to kids, he'd be nice to old people. That had to be it . . . but they were wrong. On two separate occasions, he had been called upon to change the messy diapers and bedding of patients. He had looked at the mess and thought, *Hell no!* It was easier to just put a pillow over their heads. They wiggled a little bit and presto, no mess to clean up. They'd take them out like garbage. He liked working at the nursing home . . . He liked being free. Everyone in prison said the same thing . . . Dead people don't make very good witnesses. *It was prolly the only useful thing he had learned.* It was a shame too; he'd like to keep this girl forever. He busied himself with his task. He released the nylon cord from the turnbuckle on the wall and lowered the crudely fashioned, medieval-looking set of stocks to the floor . . . *Man, she's purty,* he thought.

This is too easy, Ed thought to himself. He had told the girl to take off her clothes and put her hands and feet in the stocks and she had done so . . . like a robot. He stepped back and leaned against the wall and just stared for a long time. "Man, yur purty," he whispered. As he grabbed the rope and began to pull it through his crude, squeaky pulley system, he failed to hear the back door quietly open. Ed secured the rope on a makeshift turnbuckle he had secured to the wall when the girl's hands were stretched high above her head. He unbuckled his belt and dropped his pants. He was so caught up in the moment that he did not see the man standing in the small hallway a mere five feet away, with a shotgun leveled at his chest.

"Shame on you, Ed," the man said. Ed turned to face the man. As he did, the gun exploded. The impact slammed Ed's body against the far wall and ended his meticulously planned evening before it even got started.

Edward Hogreve slowly opened his eyes. It seemed as though every bone in his body hurt, especially his chest. As he felt his chest, he realized he was secured to the chair he was in by a thick leather strap. He tried to reposition it on his chest to ease his discomfort, but it was too tight. He tried to move his legs, but they were also secured. The good news was that his hands were free. He tried to reach around behind him to find a buckle or clasp to loosen, but he was too secure. He tried to reach the restraints on his legs but couldn't lean forward enough. As he pondered his predicament, he became aware that a bright light was focused directly on him. It reminded him of a kindergarten play he was in . . . looking out at the crowd for a familiar face as the spotlight shone brightly in his own. After a moment, he saw a man standing before him, looking through a video camera.

"State your name and the crime for which you were recently released from prison."

"I'm Ed. I killed a boy with a shovel, but they let me out cause I was good. Could you loosen up this strap? My chest is killing me."

"That's because I shot you with a forty-millimeter bean bag round. You were within lethal range. I'm glad it didn't kill you, and no, I won't loosen the strap."

"Oh," Ed said.

"Listen, Ed, I need to ask you some important questions, and it is critical that you answer them truthfully. Do you understand?"

"Yeah, I guess," Ed said.

"You raped and tortured a young girl several years ago and killed a young boy named Daniel Adkins. Why did you do that, Ed?"

Ed thought for a moment . . . Thoughts seemed to bounce around in his head like dice in a Yahtzee cup when someone shakes them too long and you almost become annoyed. Finally, a thought popped from his cup . . . "Hey, where'd that purty gurl go?"

"I suspect she's home with her parents about now."

"Oh," Ed said.

"What I need to understand, Ed, is why . . . why did you rape and torture that girl and kill the boy?"

The dice started tumbling again. "Well," Ed said, "I couldn't get a girlfriend, so I just got her."

"And the boy, why did you kill the boy?"

Ed thought again and then he smiled. "I remember. I told him to have sex with the girl so I could watch . . . And he didn't do it . . . He said he couldn't do it . . . You know what I mean?" Ed snickered and leaned forward. "He couldn't get a woody."

"So what you're telling me is that you killed Daniel Adkins because he couldn't achieve an erection. Is that right?"

Ed thought a moment, struggling to discern the meaning of "erection" and "achieve." Then he said, "Yep. I hit him with the shovel 'cause he couldn't get a woody."

Aaron turned back to the camera, adjusted the focus, and walked over to the table. He picked up a *Playboy* magazine and walked back to the chair. Standing to the right side, he handed the magazine to Ed, who seemed quite pleased at his sudden turn of fate.

The man spoke. "Ed, it's time for us to render judgment now. I'd like you to open that magazine and find a picture of a girl you like."

Ed eagerly opened the magazine. He leafed through the pages until he found Miss November. He turned the magazine around and said, "She's purty. I like her"

"Good, Ed. Do you think she is as pretty as Daniel Adkins's young female friend, the one you made your girlfriend . . . ?"

Ed looked at him like he had lost his mind. "Are you kidding me?! This woman makes that girl look like a mud hut."

"So the girl in the picture is prettier than Daniel's friend?"

'

"Good, I want to make sure I give you a fair test, equal to the test you gave Daniel."

"I didn't give him no test. I hit him with a shovel," Ed said with a you-big-dummy look.

"No, Ed, you gave him a test. You challenged him to achieve an erection under pressure. He failed. The clinical term is performance anxiety. He could not perform under pressure."

Ed's meager mental dictionary was overloaded. He seemed to hit a wall. "Hey! What do you want anyhow?"

The man stepped to the side and picked up the long-billed spade. He rested it easily on his shoulder, like Babe Ruth waiting for a pitch he liked. "What I want, Ed, is for you to look at the picture in front of you and see if you can achieve an erection. You have five minutes to do so. If you can, I will let you go. If you can't, I'm going to hit you in the face with this shovel until you're dead."

For the first time all night, Ed realized he was in trouble. The man's questions suddenly seemed to make sense. The round pegs dropped into the round holes and the square pegs in the square holes. It was like his brain was pulling out all the stops in hopes of maintaining a warm live host to reside in.

"Four minutes, Ed."

Ed grabbed for his belt buckle and unzipped his pants. As he did, he dropped the magazine. The man stooped and picked it up.

"Don't drop it again," he said. "Your life might depend on it."

Ed began fumbling with his organ with no success. He flipped the pages with such force they began to wrinkle and tear. "Oh man," he mumbled. He got to the last page and went to start over again. As he did, he lost the grip on his magazine. It fell to the floor. "Oh man!"

"Better think happy thoughts," Aaron said, "two minutes left."

The harder Ed pulled on his organ, the smaller it got, like a turtle pulling its head into its shell to avoid danger. He closed his eyes and tried to think of things that would normally stimulate his body. For the first time in his life, the tear-stained faces and cries for help turned him off instead of on.

"Time's up," Aaron said. "Edward Hogreve, justice cries out from the grave. We must answer."

Ed opened his eyes and saw the first blow come. He did not see or feel the second or third. Aaron stepped back and surveyed the scene. His eyes filled with tears as he imagined what Daniel went through, the fear that must have coursed through his body. His heart ached for the young girl that suffered at this man's hand, and it rejoiced for the young girl that was spared that night. He put down the shovel and walked to the shower. It was going to be harder than he thought. Reliving those terrible moments was like seeing the original crime as it unfolded. He wondered to himself, *Would he really want to find the man who killed his son? And experience that moment?* As Edward Hogreve's blood crawled toward the drain in the floor, Aaron slipped the DVD into a plain brown padded envelope addressed to Roberta Adkins, Return Address: IV-justice.

CHAPTER 6

Dark Angel

"HE WAS AN angel," Lindsey said for the sixth time. "I asked God to send an angel and he did."

Detective Larson stared at her a moment. She had been through a lot in the last twenty-four hours, and by the looks her father was sending him, the interview was almost over. He changed his line of questioning. "OK, Lindsey, he was an angel. What was he wearing?"

She thought for a moment, then answered, "He was wearing a black sweater."

"What kind of pants did he have on?"

"Blue jeans, I think."

"So what we have here is an angel in blue jeans and a black sweater, toting a twelve-gauge shotgun. I thought angels wore white and carried harps?" Lindsey's father leaned forward in his chair, a menacing look starting to form on his face.

Kate took the hint, and like a mother carefully removing a chocolate-covered mixer from a child who insisted on helping make frosting, Kate slowly began to clean up Jamie's mess. "Lindsey, do you remember what the first police officers who responded looked like?"

She considered the question. "They looked like cops," she said. "They had on uniforms."

"You can't remember if they were old or young, Caucasian or black?"

"I'm sorry," she said. "It was like when I wake up in the morning without contacts. There are just shapes, not clear images. It's like I didn't want to see. Does that make sense?"

"Yes it does," Kate said. "You have been through an awful lot. Just one more question, Lindsey. You said this angel killed the bad man, that he shot him."

Lindsey's eyes got big, like she was reliving the moment. "He did! He just appeared. One minute, I was alone. The next minute, he was there and he shot the man. I seen him die. He hit the wall and collapsed on to the floor just like in the movies."

"What did the angel do next?"

"He gave me a blanket and helped me get free. He said I should wait there for the police. I told him I couldn't stay there with that man even if he was dead."

"What did he say to that?" Kate asked.

"He said he would take him away, and he did!"

Kate thanked Lindsey's dad for bringing her in and gave him her card. "If she remembers anything else, please call me any time. She may start to open up and remember more details with time." He agreed. Kate walked the two of them to the front lobby.

Returning to her office, she met Jamie in the hallway with his eighth cup of coffee of the morning. "Lovely," he said, "we have a dark angel with a shotgun, dispensing justice Wild West style. Well, what the hell does an angel look like?"

"I hope he looks like Clint Eastwood or Charles Bronson," Kate said. "I'll be disappointed if he ends up looking like Ben or Jerry, the ice-cream guys."

"Aren't you funny?" Jamie said with a disapproving frown. "Even you're developing fantasies about this guy. Maybe he should run for governor like Arnold Schwarzenegger. He liked to terminate bad guys too. This prick is a cross between Robin Hood and Zorro, and I don't like it. I'm gonna nail his ass to the wall!"

"Well said, Sheriff Larson!" Kate said with a twang. "Let's hang him from a tall oak!"

Jamie glanced down at his snakeskin boots, then back at Kate. "You are impossible."

She flashed her brightest smile. "Let's ride, cowboy!" she said.

Jamie grabbed the keys from his desk and turned towards the door, not wanting her to see him smile.

Cadillac Man

The man stood and stretched, hours of watching had had made his neck stiff.

Patience, he thought, *that's what made him different from other men like him, men who acted on impulse to fulfill the desires of the moment.* He had the patience of Job. Often he had waited patiently for over a year, nurturing his fantasies like a mother hen watching over her chicks, keeping them warm and alive. Then, after what seemed like an eternity, his opportunity had come and he had acted, decisively, with the confidence that only many years of hunting could give. Now was not the time. He watched the three young boys wave goodbye to the fisherman in the boat, then take off into the "sunshiny" day, poles and bobbers bouncing from their handlebars. Maybe tomorrow it would be overcast and the boys would venture down to the dark river by themselves. Yes, time was on his side. Patience was his ally, and his intelligence was his salvation. He knew he was smarter than most of the people he conversed with as he went through his day. Often, he would not even listen to what people were saying, kind of like a speed reader reading over the fluff of the story to get at the meat of the tale. He listened for key words that related to him and his needs. Everything else was irrelevant.

He was a serial predator. His father's inheritance had allowed him to move about the country, fulfilling his carnal needs without drawing attention to himself. People don't ask a well-dressed, slightly graying middle-aged man driving a Cadillac why he's hanging on the fence at a playground watching the children. They just assumed he's keeping a watchful eye on his grandson. He had seen most states at least once and had rarely been unsuccessful. Now he was back in Michigan. He thought he'd stay awhile; this time of year was beautiful, the smell of pine in the air and the musky smell of the dark black swamps that seemed to cover half the state. He made his way back to his car. A steak and a glass of wine would have to satisfy him that night. He put the key in the ignition as a father and his son pulled in to park. As the young boy got out of the car, they made eye contact. The boy waved. The man's heart raced as he returned the friendly gesture. *Patience,* he told himself as he pulled from the curve, *Patience!*

After watching the DVD with Roberta Adkins, Jamie spoke first. "This just showed up on your doorstep?" he asked.

"Postal service dropped it off earlier today," she said. "When I came home, it was inside the door when I opened it."

"Can we see the envelope it came in?" Kate asked.

"Sure," Roberta offered and went to the kitchen to retrieve it. She returned and gave the envelope to Kate. The return address was the same as the last. IV-justice.

Jamie looked at his notes. "Roberta, have you ever been to the scene of your son's murder? I mean, to leave a memorial or offer prayers?"

"Yes, I have," she said. "Every year on the anniversary of his death, and sometimes, when I miss him really bad, I'll go up there"

"Is it hard to find?" Jamie asked.

"No," Roberta said, "it's the logging trail right across from where the old water mill used to be. Just follow it to the top of the hill. They found his body lying there on the trail. You'll see where I've put flowers every year since he died."

"One other thing, Roberta?" Jamie asked. "Do you recognize the voice on the tape? An uncle, brother, family friend, maybe"

"No," Roberta said, "I've asked myself that same question. The voice seems familiar in some generic way, like a car salesman, or an insurance agent, maybe a therapist, that's it. I've seen a few of those over the last six years."

She stopped like she was lost in thought. Kate and Jamie waited for her to speak. "But there was something in his voice that sounded familiar. The flatness of it, it was like he didn't want to kill that man, but he had to. He sounded . . . he sounded . . . like . . . like I would sound if I were asking the questions and holding the shovel. Maybe he is the father of a murdered child. Have you considered that?"

"That is one of the things we've considered," Jamie said.

"I'm sorry you had to see this DVD, Miss Adkins. It must have been hard. We are doing our best to capture the man responsible."

Roberta looked at Jamie for a long time before she spoke, like she was trying see into the recesses of his heart and know his true feelings. Finally she spoke. "Detective Larson, I pay my taxes. I believe in God and country, right and wrong. But I also believe in the bond between a mother and her child. There is no bond more absolute. It's like the law of gravity. When my son was murdered, I died inside.

My heart was fractured, torn, ruined. It's hard to explain the loss in words. But this man, this vigilante, they call him, has given my life back to me. He has made my life as good as it can be without Daniel. I no longer have to worry about where Daniel's killer is, or who he might hurt next. I'm no longer concerned about why the justice system let him go after killing my son. And most of all, I don't need to worry about what I might do if I seen him walking down the street. And make no mistake, if I could have swung that shovel myself, Detective Larson, *by God, I would have*! So you find this man, arrest him, and convict him, but before you send him to prison, you pin a medal on his chest and you thank him for Roberta Adkins!"

Neither Jamie nor Kate spoke for a long time after the sobering speech from Roberta. "Where to now?" Kate asked.

"The Lost Nation's Wildlife Area," Jamie said. "I've got a hunch." Kate knew better than to second guess Jamie's hunches, so she settled back for the drive south. They stopped at the Pittsford Carry-out to use the bathroom and grab a Coke before making the final drive down to the old mill. Shadows were stretching across the mill pond as they parked on the old logging trail. "Come on," Jamie said, "we only have about an hour of daylight left." Kate radioed their location to dispatch and got out of the car. The spring rains had left the trail quite eroded and very slippery. They carefully made their way up the hill, looking for pieces of rock or patches of grass to help gain a foothold. As they crested the top of the hill and found level ground, they both stopped for a breather. Kate saw the body first and motioned to Jamie, almost afraid to speak out loud, for fear she might wake the apparition in front of them. Jamie walked closer, careful not to disturb any evidence. Leaning against an old pine tree was the body of Edward Hogreve. At least, that's who Jamie suspected it was. Only fingerprints would tell for sure, because the body in front of them had no discernable face. In his lap were six bouquets of flowers in various stages of decomposition. He looked like a florist on his way to the zombie prom. Carved in his bare chest was the number "IV" and the word "justice."

After dropping the boys at their bikes, Aaron secured the boat in the slip he rented for the summer, got in the truck, and headed for home. He had taken up fishing after his son had died, mostly because his son had always wanted to go and they had rarely gotten the chance. His construction schedule during the summer months was exhausting and left little time for leisure. *What was the old saying? "Make hay while the sun is shining." It should be: "Catch fish while your son is living."*

He quickly checked that negative thought; too many of those would throw him into a tailspin again. And he could not afford to let that happen. The papers were starting to dub him the Gatekeeper. The *Ann Arbor Times* said that if Saint Peter welcomes good people into heaven, then the Gatekeeper ushers pedophiles into hell. The nickname had stuck like glue. Aaron Reynolds was the Gatekeeper, a job he planned to keep for a long time or until the ache in his heart went away for good. He went in his house and made a sandwich. He called Susan, "Hey, sweetie," she answered before he said a word.

"Is that woman's intuition?" Aaron asked.

"Don't flatter yourself, darling. It's called caller ID, but I have been waiting for your number to pop up, if that makes you feel better."

"It does," he said. "Want to go out tonight?"

"Let me look at my schedule and I'll get back to you," she said.

He pulled the phone away from his ear and looked at it like it had somehow malfunctioned. He heard her laughing.

"Of course, Aaron, I'd love to. What time?"

"Say 7:00 p.m.? Susan, do you mind if I invite Libby and Raymond? I'll see if they can get a sitter for little Ray."

"Sounds like fun. See you at 7:00, handsome."

He had met Susan a year earlier at a victims' rights banquet. She and her sister had suffered abuse at the hands of their stepfather for years. They had both come to terms with their abuse and had since worked tirelessly to help other victims of violent crime. She was a wonderful, mature woman, with a great sense of humor. Aaron adored her and cherished the times they spent together; he never once had the feeling she was a gold-digger. They both seemed to feel the same way about each other. They were comfortable in their own skins and content to remain that way.

Libby waved her father and Susan over to their table. She and Raymond had arrived at Savorino's early and found a quaint table near the rear. She smiled as she watched them thread their way through the maze of tables. She was so proud of her father. He had overcome so much adversity, and now he was content and happy again. After exchanging greetings all around, they settled down to a wonderful meal. Libby brought Aaron up to date on the current status of Reynolds & Reynolds while Raymond seemed content to expound on Ray Jr's batting average and overall athletic skill sets. Aaron exchanged glances with Susan. They seemed to be reading each other's minds. *Been there, done that,* was the thought of the moment.

Aaron struggled to gain a foothold in the conversation. "Seen little Ray today," he said proudly. "Took him and two buddies out on the river rock bass fishing. Actually, I spent more time rigging poles than fishing, but it was still a great time. They love going out on the boat. We fished till we ran out of hooks. Then I dropped them at the boat ramp, and they headed for high ground on their sting rays. Oh, to be a kid again," he said wistfully. "A swift bike, a stiff pole, and a Daisy BB gun."

"Don't start that BB gun business again, Dad," Libby smiled.

"Sorry, honey, I promised little Ray I'd try a flanking maneuver."

"Well, you're not going to breach my defenses that easily, Father."

"No, I don't suppose so," he said, winking at his son-in-law.

Libby frowned at her husband, who was torn between impressing his father-in-law and pleasing his wife, both of whom waited quietly to see what his take was on the matter. He finally threw back his shoulders and spoke with all the authority he could muster, "Waiter! Check please!"

CHAPTER 7

The Gatekeeper

Cadillac Man

THE WARM SPRING air blew in the windows along with the sounds of the small town, dogs barking, people talking, an occasional horn honking, and the mix on the radio only added to the sense of well-being. Lynyrd Skynyrd rocked, and Bonnie Raitt crooned as he drove through town, past the bakery and the stop-and-go. *What a wonderful place to live and raise a family! What was the name of this place? Saline . . . Saline, that's it, Saline, Michigan. Just a skip from the big city of Detroit but miles removed in atmosphere and pace.* A CNN news bulletin interrupted John Forgery's classic tune *Oh Suzy–Q.*

The illusive Gatekeeper had claimed his third victim in fifteen months, the report said. The man turned the radio up and pulled his car into a parking spot in front of his destination. Nathanial Higgins's body was discovered behind the Olive Branch Church near Ypsilanti, Michigan, Tuesday. The coroner ruled his death a homicide due to asphyxiation, with a post-mortem gunshot wound to the head. Higgins had long been the prime suspect in the slaying of fourteen-year-old Debra Marie Fredrickson, whose body was found two years earlier in the same location. Police reports stated that she had a clear plastic bag duct-taped over her head and her hands were duct taped behind her back when found. The body was located after an anonymous tip was received by the Ypsilanti Sheriff's Department. Handwriting samples found imprinted on a legal notepad obtained at Higgins's residence matched those of a last will and testament written by Miss Fredrickson. In the heart-wrenching document, she addressed her parents, telling them not to let her death ruin their lives, that she had peace and knew God was with her. She said her abductor told her that he would have to kill her to keep his identity a secret, but he had grown to like her so he wanted to give her the option to die by asphyxiation or gunshot, both of which he claimed would be painless. Autopsy reports revealed that Frederickson died by asphyxiation and had been sexually assaulted. Higgins, a well-known and previously convicted sex offender and neighbor of the victim, was never charged with the crime. District Attorney James Watts said his office was reluctant to file charges against Higgins without further evidence. An undisclosed similar MO prompted the Detroit Metro Special Crimes Unit's lead detective, James Larson, to attribute the crime to the Gatekeeper. The report went on to say: "It looks as if the Gatekeeper offered the same deal to Higgins that Higgins offered to his young victim, with one exception. Higgins's body was found with a clear plastic bag duct-taped over his head and a single post-mortem gunshot wound to the forehead. Now back to your regularly scheduled program. This is Rick Dean. You're listening to WLKZ. Sounds like the bad guy got the two for one deal, a bag and a bullet. Go, Gatekeeper! And now, back to the top fifty greatest hits of all time. At number 23, the Rolling Stones classic 'I Can't Get No Satisfaction!'"

The man considered the lyrics of the song. Jaeger's frustrating ballad coupled with his own lack of satisfaction caused him to turn the radio off and hit the recline button on his seat. He sat there for some time watching the children. The sign in the window said: "The Ice Cream Dream." Below, in cursive letters, it said: "We all dream of *ice cream*" He pondered their catchphrase for a moment as he lowered his window. Without being conspicuous, he slowly lifted his nose to the breeze. He could smell them, like newborn fawns or rabbits, fresh and unmolested. *Not everyone dreams of ice cream,* he thought.

He eased the shiny Cadillac out on to the main drag and slowly headed east toward the memorial park. The town constable waved at him, clearly pleased to have the big shiny car in his small pathetic town. He returned the gesture. *Cops,* he thought, *so predictable. This Gatekeeper, though, who was he? What was he? A rogue cop? A grieving parent? I hope they catch him soon,* he laughed to himself. *He sounds like a desperate, dangerous man.*

Jamie and Kate waited nervously in Captain Wells's office. He entered red-faced and sweating profusely, like usual. He sat down and kicked his feet up on the desk. "So," he said, "what do you have for me? Tell me something good!"

Jamie looked at Kate like she held the Holy Grail of information. Captain Wells followed his gaze. "About what?" Kate said.

"The Gatekeeper!" the captain growled. "Tell me you have some leads, please? I have a press conference in one hour. The whole country is watching this case."

Jamie spoke first, "Captain, we have a tremendous caseload right now. I doubt if we are devoting ten hours a week to this case. Every officer I talk to says, 'Let him work his magic. He's doing us a favor.' It personally grinds my ass that he's killing these dirtbags with impunity, but I seem to be the minority. Even Kate here would like his autograph."

Kate's face seemed to transform like the girl in the *Exorcist*, and Jamie didn't know whether to cross himself or run. The captain realized his predicament and slammed his fist down on the desk. "You two shut the hell up and listen to me. I'm going to go out there in one hour and tell those reporters that I've formed a task force, effective today, to apprehend the Gatekeeper and put an end to these vigilante-style killings. I'm going to tell them that I'm putting Detective James Larson in charge, with Special Agent Kate Wagner in charge of inter-agency communications." They both sat up straighter at the sound of their new titles.

"How many men will we have, sir?" Jamie asked. Kate was already relishing the thought of verbally bullying half a dozen young male detectives.

"Two!" the captain said. "You and Kate. You are the Gatekeeper Task Force. Give Bill the rest of your caseload and work exclusively on this. There will be another briefing on Wednesday. That gives you five days to come up with something. Now hit the bricks. No shit! Move!"

Kate and Jamie tried to go through the door at the same time, anxious to get out of the captain's zone of influence. They hurried out the back way to the parking garage. As they pulled into traffic, Jamie said, "Let's go to O'Brien's and brainstorm, maybe have a frosted mug of green beer. Isn't it close to Saint Patrick's Day?"

"Are you asking me on a date?" Kate said.

"No, I'm asking you if you'll buy me a beer and chicken wings. I left my wallet at home."

"Sure," Kate said, trying to mask her disappointment.

The remnants of a second dozen wings sat cooling in their sticky sauce as Kate watched Jamie down his second very large pitcher of green liquid cheer. He winked at her and smiled. "Maybe this is a date after all," he said.

"Fat chance, cowboy. This is a tacky establishment, with tacky food and tacky beer. This would be a great place to bring a bimbo, maybe have sex in the truck afterwards. Well, I'm not a bimbo. I'm a lady, in case you haven't noticed!"

Haven't noticed? Jamie thought, *Who hasn't noticed?* But he played along. "I'm sorry," he said. "It's just that your big 357 revolver is so unladylike, makes a man question his masculinity." He pointed his finger at her and cocked his imaginary trigger, "Go ahead, make my day!"

"You said you liked my gun!" she said, clearly offended.

"I do," he said, "in the same way I like howitzers and bunker-busting bombs. Men love overkill. I mean, size matters. Right?"

"Only when it comes to brains!" Kate said and got her wallet out to pay the bill.

Kate dropped Jamie at his house and drove off without saying a word. He figured he'd apologize later when his s's didn't sound like z's. "Zorry, Kaddy, would prolly make things worse." They hadn't accomplished much at their brainstorming session, so he went inside and sat at the computer. As the green beer evaporated from his pores, an idea germinated in the green-grey matter of his brain. He went to the National Sex Offender's Registration Web site, clicked on Michigan, and started to search. *This might work,* he thought. In five minutes, he found the names and addresses of all three of the Gatekeeper's victims. *This has to be the source of his information,* he thought. He cursed the green ale. He would like to bounce his idea off the captain, but did not yet trust his ability to string words together. He continued his search as the idea in his mind became a small green bud.

The boys grabbed their poles and peddled furiously for the river. *Grandpa Aaron said he didn't want to take the boat out in this wind, said it would be hard to keep steady. He said it wasn't a good day for fishing because the wind was out of the east.* "Wind from the east, fish bite the least," he said. Little Ray knew that was just a grown-up way of saying, "I don't want to go fishing today." So they decided to fish off the boat docks. They only had a dozen crickets and no worms, but they might find a fat little salamander under a rock near the bank after they were done fishing. Maybe that big black water snake would be prowling around. He took the lead and peddled harder as he thought of the possibilities the day might bring. He hoped no one would be in their spot when they got there. Sometimes, high school kids came down to throw stones in the river and kiss girls. *I'd rather throw stones at girls and kiss a fish,* he thought!

The river looked black under the overcast sky as the boys crested the hill, only adding to its mystical pull. Their spot was empty. "Woo hoo!" he yelled. The whole park was empty, except for the guy in the fancy car, and he never fished anyway. Ray thought he probably wanted to be a little boy again and catch fish himself, because all he ever did was watch them. If they had worms, he might consider inviting the man down to catch a fish with his pole.

"So how you feeling?" Kate hollered as she waited for Jamie to get out of the shower. She had let herself in after he failed to appear on the front porch that morning like he usually did, with his cup of coffee in one hand and paper in the other. No answer. "Hey!" she yelled. "You alive in there"

"I'm sorry," he said, sounding ever so contrite.

"For what?" Kate said.

"For anything I don't remember saying or doing and for half of the things I do remember."

"No problem. I'm a hard-core, flat-chested bitch, remember? I have no feelings."

Jamie threw open the door, a towel wrapped around his waist. "Did I say that? Please, Katie, tell me I didn't say that!" Kate tried to keep a straight face but couldn't. She lost it. Jamie was so relieved that he hadn't committed the infraction that he didn't mind being the butt of her joke. "OK, funny," he said. "Listen! I have a plan. It has a lot of holes in it, but I think it will work. What if we try and draw the Gatekeeper out into the open? If the captain OKs it, we'll register me with a fictitious name on the National Sex Offender's Registry as just returning from prison after an overturned conviction because of some bullshit technical mistake by the district attorney. We'll rent one of those furnished apartments down on East Jackson for two weeks. I'll sit in the house and watch TV for two weeks and you can do surveillance. Get the license number of every car that comes down that back street. We'll run all the plates and see if we can shake something loose, kind of like a vacation. Cap said we can devote all our time to this one."

"Let me get this straight," Kate said. "You watch TV while I sit in a hot car and do surveillance. For how long each day?"

"Say from noon till nine. That's an hour overtime every day for two weeks. The rest of the time, I'll cover myself. Get yourself a good book to read. We'll get a couple of hundred plates to run and give the Cap his golden nugget for the next press conference."

Kate sighed and dialed the captain's number. "Hello, Captain Wells? This is Kate Wagner, Director in Charge of Inter-agency Communications with the Gatekeeper Task Force. I'd like to announce a major development in the Gatekeeper case. We are about to launch a major undercover operation with Special Agent James Larson spearheading the sting."

The line went silent for a moment, then Kate heard, "Nice! Sounds like bullshit, but I can sell it. What's your plan?"

Cadillac Man

The man opened his trunk and took out a small duffel bag. He took one last look around before heading down to the dock. He walked easily, without glancing nervously about. As he got closer, one of the boys looked up and waved. He smiled and walked closer. *Patience,* he told himself. "Any luck?" the man asked.

"Not much," one of the boys said. "All we have is crickets and rock bass, like worms."

"Yes, they do," the man said. "I used to use willow worms and caught a fish on almost every cast."

All three heads spun towards him in unison, like he had just announced Free Candy Day at the Five & Dime. "Willow worms!" Little Ray said. "Where we can buy those?"

"Oh, you can't buy them," the man said. "You have to dig 'em up." All three boys were standing around him in a semicircle now, like moths gathering to the light. "The only place to dig up a willow worm is under a willow tree," the man said. "Like those down there." He pointed to a willow grove about two hundred yards downriver, their branches hanging low to the ground like a great skirt hiding their bare trunks.

"Don't we need a shovel?" little Ray asked.

"Nope, the ground under a willow is soft. You can dig it with a stick. That's why the worms like it there. I could help you boys dig some if you let me catch a fish with you."

Little Ray spoke for the group. "Mister, you help us get some willow worms, and I'll let you catch five fish."

"Let's go," one of the boys urged. "We gotta get them worms!"

They all three started for the willow grove.

"Hey!" the man said. "You don't want to leave your poles and bikes here, do ya? Some teenager is likely to run off with them."

"Oh yeah! Thanks, mister," Ray said as they grabbed their gear and headed out, pushing their bikes at a more leisurely pace. The man strolled along behind them, being careful not to let the sexual tension in him stiffen his gait.

CHAPTER 8

Undercover

AARON REGRETTED HAVING to turn Little Ray down on their Saturday fishing trip, but preparations had to be made for his next visitor to the chamber. Donny Wheeler, recently released from prison because of an overturned conviction for the rape and strangulation of a six-year-old boy, could possibly pose a threat to his own grandson. Residing on the east side of Ann Arbor, in the East Jackson Street Apartments, he was less than twelve miles as the crow flies from Libby and Raymond's home. *Too close,* he thought as he walked outside and removed the battery charger from the old Econoline van, the last relic of his former construction company. He took the current plate sticker out of his wallet and affixed it to the fifteen-year-old plate, jumped in, and turned the key. The old engine roared to life like it had been waiting all those years for another chance to serve. He pulled an old baseball cap low over his eyes and headed into town. He felt invisible in the rusty old van with the barely visible R&D construction logo on the side, just another struggling carpenter trying to build a future with his hammer. He pulled into the hardware store and went inside. He asked the clerk for a motion-activated air freshener.

She led him to the back wall. After taking a quick visual inventory, she relayed her findings to Aaron. "We have three models," she said, "two battery-powered and one that plugs into a receptacle."

"Well," Aaron said, "it needs to be battery-operated and it needs to have a refillable reservoir."

"This is the one!" She held the package up and smiled. She read the back. "The spray is adjustable from two to seven seconds, motion-activated, refillable reservoir, and battery-powered."

"Bingo," Aaron said. "Thank you for your help."

She smiled and shooed him toward the checkout counter. He made his purchase and headed for the door. Outside, he climbed in the old van and drove toward the east side of town.

He drove slowly, like he was looking for a home that was in need of a roof repair. Apartment 115 was the downstairs apartment of a duplex. It had a driveway that led right to the front door. In the driveway sat an old maroon Buick Century. Aaron noted the plate number and continued on. He went around the block and cased the immediate neighborhood. He soon found what he was looking for, a 7-11 party store two blocks away. The next closest was six blocks away. He thought to himself, *What does every pedophile need besides children?* Beer and cigarettes. He backed his old van into a parking spot in the rear of the carry out and settled in for a long wait. He looked at his watch. Six o'clock in the evening, he hoped to establish a pattern for old Donny boy.

Cadillac Man

The man heard the loud engine before he saw the car-load of teenagers and immediately did a 360 and walked casually back towards his Cadillac. The Camaro crested the hill just as he made his way to the parking lot. He stretched, took out a cigarette. He lit it as the car full of kids rumbled past. The passenger nodded to the man. He did not acknowledge the gesture but glanced toward the willows, just as the boys parted the willows' yellow-green skirt and disappeared within. He was raging inside, *So close!* Slowly, he gained his composure. He waited five minutes to see if the teens might move on. He might still be satisfied. But he soon smelled hemp on the breeze and knew the night was over. He pulled slowly out of the park. The next day, he would go back to Saline and shake up their quiet town.

Kate noted the plate number of the old construction van and put it at the bottom of her list. Jamie told her to put all service vehicles and city trucks at the bottom and all domestic autos and trucks at the top. Any suspicious vehicles were to get a check mark beside them. She already had sixty-four check marks on her sheet, and it was only the fourth day. Everyone in this neighborhood looked suspicious. At 9:00 p.m., she flashed her lights once, and the front porch light on the house blinked once in return, telling Kate all was well and she could go home and get some sleep. After Kate drove past, Jamie waited a half hour, then went out and got in the old Buick they had borrowed from the impound lot. He drove to the 7-11. He let the car idle out front and went inside. He grabbed a Bud Select tall boy, a pack of Camels, and went back to the car. *If he was gonna be cooped up for two weeks, at least he'd have one beer a night. After all, this was kind of like a vacation.*

Hello, Donny, Aaron said to himself as he peered through the windshield of the old van at the Buick parked out front, *do you do this every night at nine thirty? I sure hope so. This could work out very nicely.* Jamie left the parking lot and went straight back to the house. He felt less vulnerable inside four walls, especially posing as a pedophile. He watched CSI and hit the rack. He had put a dead bolt on the only door, so he rested easy with his service revolver at his side.

For the next five days, he was never out of the house for more than ten minutes each day and was always back by nine forty-five so he didn't miss his favorite program at ten. He knew Kate would be furious if she knew he was slipping out each evening to get a beer, so he kept her in the dark about his nightly forays. She had already logged over two hundred plates, so their operation was already a success.

On the sixth night at 1:00 a.m., Aaron pulled on to a side street near Jamie's duplex and got out of the van. He strolled easily through the rundown neighborhood. It was Sunday night, and the work week would start in the morning, so all of the working class were settled in for the night and the criminal elements had closed up shop to sleep off their hangovers from Friday and Saturday. So the streets were mostly deserted. He strolled casually down the side street, trying to stay in the shadows wherever possible. He paused in front of Apartment 115. The curtains were pulled and the house was dark. Slowly, he eased up the driveway, being careful to step on the grass and not make noise in the gravel. He quietly opened the door of the old Buick and sat in the driver's seat. He took the paper off the adhesive strip and attached the air freshener to the visor just above the driver's head. He turned the switch on, got out, and quickly closed the driver's door. He made his way back to the street, retraced his steps to the van, and drove slowly back to the farm.

He went to the chamber and started making preparations. He opened the blood pressure cuff he had ordered online and looked it over. It was oversized, designed for obese individuals. He wrapped it around his thigh, just above his knee and squeezed the rubber bulb. A steady constant pressure began to stop the flow of blood to his calf. He removed the short rubber hose and replaced it with a twenty-foot long piece of vacuum line he had purchased at the auto parts store. *This should work nicely,* he thought to himself, pleased with the progress the last twenty-four hours had yielded.

Monday passed uneventfully and Kate flashed her lights at nine o'clock. The porch light came on and stayed on. She slowly drove past the apartment; Jamie stepped out the door and picked up the paper that was deposited earlier that afternoon. As he stood up, he blew her a kiss and winked at her. She almost hit a garbage can but managed a quick evasive maneuver at the last second. She looked back to see if Jamie had seen her blunder, but he was already in the house. *Thank goodness,* she breathed, *I'd hate for that man to know he pushes my buttons. He would play me like a fiddle.* Jamie waited until nine thirty and headed for the door. The weather was warm, so he unclipped the service revolver from his belt and put the small twenty-five in his sock. That allowed him to leave his jacket off and fly his greasy wife-beater. *The pedophiles' uniform of choice,* he thought as he opened the Buick's door. He slid into the driver's seat and heard a small metallic click. A red light appeared in his peripheral vision and a quick discharge of moist toxic air hit him directly in his face. His mind's eye painted the picture of an angry white tom cat with one red eye. "Hissss," he heard as everything went black.

At nine forty-five, Aaron backed his van up beside the maroon Buick. He got out and opened a sliding door. He was thankful that Donny had attempted to open the door of the Buick before succumbing to the chloroform. It gave the gas a chance to dissipate so Aaron could handle his limp package without the bulky gas mask. Even so, he held his breath as he heaved his cargo into the van. He quickly secured his hands and feet with nylon tie wraps and put a cloth bag over his head. He eased the van out of the rundown neighborhood, feeling like one of those animal wranglers on public television who just successfully removed a pesky gator or snake from the neighborhood.

Cadillac Man

The man sat in the Saline Memorial Park for three hours, watching the children as the evening sun began to set. He watched them carefully as one by one, they began to leave, like a great lion watches a herd of gazelles, waiting for one with a weakness to wander away from the herd. One boy was so mesmerized by his radio-controlled monster truck that he seemed oblivious to the exodus and the lateness of the hour and was soon all by himself. The man studied his prey. His shirt was dirty and his sneakers were well worn. The truck he was happily following toward the dark end of the park had been duct-taped together numerous times. He did the mental calculations in his head and ran a risk/reward spreadsheet in his mind. No one would look for this boy until after dark. That was two hours away. After his failure the night before at the boat ramp and his fitful night without sleep, he was sure even a short violent encounter would be very gratifying. He slipped on a pair of brown jersey gloves and removed the sharp survival knife from his duffel bag. He got quietly out of the car and walked stiffly toward the boy at a quick pace. He sensed the change coming over him again like it always did, a great heat in his belly that over-rode rational thought. That's why he was so careful in his scouting and preparation. Once he released himself to this bloodlust, his mind would have no control until his lust was satisfied. This was no fresh fawn, more like a sacrificial goat. But it would calm him and allow him to think more clearly. It would allow him to be patient again and wait for an opportunity to spend more time with his victim, in a place of his choosing, like he had with the boy from Lincoln.

Jamie seemed to hover between fantasy and reality. He dreamed of a great white, red-eyed cat, hissing in his face vile, wet, antiseptic vapor. His head was spinning. When he opened his eyes, the spinning stopped, but bile rose in his stomach. When he closed his eyes, the nausea retreated but his head began to spin again. This back-and-forth tug of war continued until a voice called to him from far away. "Donny Wheeler?"

"Yes," he said without thinking.

"State the crime you were recently released from prison for."

Years of undercover training worked to his disadvantage in this drugged stupor as he quickly recited his cover story from memory. "They say I strangled a boy, but I'm innocent," Donny/Jamie said, still not able to get a grasp on reality.

"That's what we are going to try and figure out," Aaron said, "so we can render justice."

Jamie surfaced for a moment and said, "I don't think I really killed a boy. I'm just pretending I killed a boy . . ."

"Why would you do that?" Aaron said.

Jamie struggled for an answer that would not come. "I don't know," he said. "Why would I do that?"

"Try to think," Aaron said as he squeezed the bulb in his hand slowly, applying pressure to the cuff wrapped around Jamie's neck.

Jamie felt the sudden pressure build in his head and the lack of oxygen seemed to clear his mind as he choked out . . . "I'm a cop, that's why. I pretended to kill a boy. I'm a cop."

Aaron released the pressure. "That's a new one. The problem is the boy is still dead, whether you pretended to kill him or not. Justice cries out from the grave," Aaron said. "We must answer." Aaron squeezed the bulb ten times very quickly, effectively shutting off Jamie's oxygen completely. His eyes bulged and Kate's face seemed to call to him.

"Jamie," she said, "are you there? Hello, Jamie!"

The pressure released and his mind was clear, crystal clear. "I'm Detective James Larson. I'm in charge of the Gatekeeper Task Force. I'm *undercover!*" He could not see the man's face for the bright light in his own, but he felt the pressure release and sensed a change in the air.

"You're an officer?"

"Yes, Special Crimes Unit . . . Detroit Metro Police Department. My name is James Larson. We set up a fictitious name on the Sex Offender's Registration Web site to try and draw out the Gatekeeper."

Aaron was not sure he believed the man's story. He walked over to a table where his police band radio sat and picked up a chart. He walked back and stood behind the light, careful now not to let his face be shown. "If you're a police officer, what does Code 10-0 mean?"

"Use caution," Jamie said.

"And Code 10-54, what does that mean?"

"Suspicious vehicle."

Aaron pondered his predicament. "One final question, Officer Larson. What does Code 30 mean?"

Jamie sighed and hung his head. "Officer needs assistance." Jamie waited as the man seemed to consider his answers.

Soon the man stepped forward, but his face was obscured by a chemical mask of some kind. He walked up and stood in front of Jamie. He held up the air freshener, a red light came on, and Jamie heard a familiar metallic click. He turned his head as the angry red-eyed cat hissed in his face for the second time that night.

Damn that cat! he thought as he drifted off.

CHAPTER 9

Sweet Disclosure

KATE KNOCKED ON the door. "Jamie, are you there? Hello, Jamie!" Kate knew instantly that something was wrong. She had arrived at noon to start her shift, and Jamie had failed to come out of the house and give her the predetermined all's-well signal, a cigarette on the steps in the morning sun. Her heart stopped as she considered the possibilities. There was only one reason Jamie didn't come out! Because he couldn't come out. She tried the door. Locked! She busted the glass with her revolver and reached inside. After pulling back the dead bolt, she slowly opened the door and entered the house. She cleared the kitchen, then proceeded through the house, one room at a time to the living room. She found his revolver lying on his jacket. *Not good,* she thought. She was sure that Jamie had not spent an hour away from his service weapon in the last twenty years. She took out her phone and called Captain Wells. After briefing him on the situation, she went outside to check out the Buick. Something caught her attention as she neared the car. The grass was flattened where a heavy vehicle of some kind had backed up in the yard next to the Buick. Her heart sank. Jamie was gone, taken, a twenty-five-year veteran of the force snatched out from under her nose. He had not fired a shot or struggled in any way. She opened the door and slid into the car. An unmistakable medicinal smell assaulted her nose. She quickly got out of the car and took a deep breath of fresh air. Her eyes blurred, then came back into focus. *Chloroform!* she said to herself.

As she waited for the crime scene techs, she walked across the street and started canvassing the neighborhood for information. She spent the rest of the morning trying to find anyone who had seen anything the night before, hoping against hope that an eyewitness would come forward with information about her missing partner. *Or was he more?* she thought to herself. Was it more than a professional bond she felt? She remembered the kiss he had blown her only last night and the effect it had on her. Did he know how she felt about him? Did she show him? Would he ever know?

She made a promise to herself that when she found him, and she would, she would show him exactly how she felt.

Cadillac Man

Libby Reynolds awaited her next client, a Mr. Evan McGregor. He had called their office earlier that week and asked if one of their reps could broker the sale of some stocks from his father's estate, stocks that his father had held for almost fifty years, Procter & Gamble and General Electric. He said he hadn't a clue what they were worth, but he wanted to raise capital to purchase a home in Florida for his retirement. After reviewing the potential sale, protocol required that Libby broker the deal because of the high dollar amount and the possible financial liability to the company.

"Mrs Reynolds, Mr. McGregor is here to see you"

"Thank you, Mary. Send him in please." Libby invited the man to have a seat and thanked him for choosing Reynolds & Reynolds to handle his financial needs.

"Well," Evan said, "you seem to have the market cornered when it comes to brokering a deal of this size. All of your competitors just shook their heads and recommended your firm. I guess the zeros scared them away."

"To be truthful, Mr. McGregor, there are not many firms in town prepared to cut a check for 2.6 million dollars even though there is a substantial commission. The numbers can be a little sobering."

"Are you serious?!" Evan exclaimed. "I had no idea they were worth that much! My father really knew how to pick 'em!"

"Yes, he did," Libby agreed. "It should make you a very comfortable retirement fund."

"Oh," Evan said, "it's not for my retirement fund. It's for a house in the Keys. My father set up my retirement account when I was born, and it has become quite a monstrosity. It's ridiculous, really. I've never had to work. I've never known what a true friend is, and female companionship is almost out of the question. I'm afraid they will trip when we go on a date and sue me for a mill. Anyway, thank you for your time and for helping me navigate these financial waters. If I have any needs in the future, I will certainly let your firm handle things for me."

Libby showed him to the door. As he was leaving, she asked him how long he thought he might be in the area?

"I'll probably stick around until fall, do some hunting, then head south with the snow birds."

"Whitetail hunting?" Libby asked.

"Excuse me?" Evan said with a quizzical look.

"Whitetail deer? Are you going to be hunting deer? We have way more than our share, you know."

"Yes," Evan said, ". . . deer . . . that's what I'll be hunting."

Odd, Libby thought, *what kind of hunter didn't know what a whitetail was?* "Probably the rich, spoiled kind," she said to herself as Evan left her office.

The maroon Cadillac pulling away from the front of the Reynolds & Reynolds office building looked oddly familiar to Aaron as he pulled into his executive parking space in the front lot. Little Ray also took notice. "That's the worm guy," he proclaimed!

"Who's the worm guy?" Aaron said.

"The guy in the shiny car. He told us we could find worms under the willow trees down by the river, but the ground was too hard. We needed a shovel. I told him we would, but he said noo, use a stick. He offered to help us, but then he didn't even help."

Aaron remembered seeing the Cadillac down by the boat docks on numerous occasions. He looked at Little Ray, trying to piece together his story. "Ray, you and I dig worms all the time. You don't need help getting worms."

"These kind you do," Ray said. "These are willow worms," he said. "We needed willow worms to catch rock bass."

Aaron put the car in park and turned off the engine. He turned to Little Ray and said, "Raymond, tell me about the worm guy. Start from the beginning."

The cruiser slowly made its way through the park past the ball diamonds and shelter houses. As it neared the playground, it slowed to a stop in front of a park bench.

On the bench, a vagrant man lay sleeping or dead, face covered with a newspaper. It was almost noon. And the sun should have already caused the body to bloat or wake, depending on its status in the land of the living. The window on the cruiser came down slowly. Still no movement. "Hey, buddy, move it along. Rise and shine. Getty up." Still no movement. The two officers looked at each other with rising alarm, neither rookie having dealt with a stiff before. They got out of the car and walked over to the man.

"Whew, smells like he crapped himself."

"That's the last thing you do before you die," the other officer said.

"*I'm not dead*" the man said through the newspaper, sending both officers bolting for the car before they caught themselves and tried to regain their composure. Jamie pulled the newspaper from his face and blinked into the noonday sun. His head felt like it was going to explode. He slowly sat up and stared at the two cherry cops. "Boo!" he said. They both did a good Barney Fife imitation, and Jamie started to laugh. "Big mistake! Ouch," he groaned, "don't make me laugh. My head is killing me."

The bravest of the two stuck his thumbs in his belt and took two steps toward Jamie, then a half step back, trying to maintain what he felt was a safe distance.

Jamie tired of the game and said, "Calm down there, bub. I'm an officer. I'm undercover!"

The two cops looked at each other like he just announced he was Santa Claus. They both started to laugh. The brave one said, "You don't smell like a cop."

The other mustered up the courage to speak for the first time, "Yeah, whacha trying to do? Catch a garbage man?"

Jamie looked at the two rookies for a long time before he decided against taking them out and driving their cruiser to the house. "Give me your phone," he said to the brave cop. "*Give it to me!*" he yelled!

Kate answered the phone on the first ring, recognizing the number as that of a city unit and hoping for news of Jamie.

"Hey, girly," Jamie said, "can you meet me at my place in an hour? I'll tell you what I've been up to."

"You'll tell me right this minute," Kate replied.

"Please, Katie, you have no idea how bad my head hurts. Don't argue with me right now. See you in one hour? Call the captain. Tell him I'm fine. I'll need a day or so off. Can you do that for me, please?"

Kate remembered the promise she made to herself and her voice softened, "Sure, pard. I'll see you in an hour and Jamie"

"What?" Jamie asked.

"Never mind. I'll see you in an hour."

It seemed like two hours had passed when Kate pulled into Jamie's drive. While she waited for the prescribed hour, she had gone home and freshened up, put on her favorite jeans and top. She left her unfeminine 357 revolver under the seat and locked the car. She knocked twice and left herself in. The bathroom door was closed and the shower was running again. She walked up to the door and, in her best Marilyn Monroe voice, said, "Sweetheart, we've got to stop meeting like this."

Jamie opened the door, pulled her close, and kissed her long and hard. She was so stunned by his advance that she failed to respond to him. He held her face and looked into her eyes. "Last night, I was dying, Katie, and I seen your face. You called to me. You wouldn't let me die. I don't know how you feel about me, Katie, but I think I love you. I thought I was going to die without ever being able to tell you that. Working with you all these years, being so close, and never touching you, I need you, Kate. I want you. I don't want to look at you longingly any more."

Kate looked at him like she was seeing him for the first time. "You need me?" she said.

"Uh-huh . . ."

"You want me? . . ."

"Uh-huh . . ."

She smiled, took his hand in hers, and led him towards the bedroom. "I had something I wanted to tell you, Jamie . . . but I think I'll just show you instead."

Aaron and Little Ray meet Libby in the reception area. They planned to have lunch downtown at the food court. Aaron kissed his daughter, and Little Ray hugged her and kissed her, not wanting to be outdone by Grandpa.

"Wow!" Libby said, "Lunch with two handsome fellows. What a lucky girl I am!"

Little Ray smiled and Aaron led the way to the car. They drove downtown as Libby filled them in on the first half of her day. She was excited to tell her father about her last client, Mr. Evan McGregor.

"Yes," Aaron said, "I think I seen him leaving as we pulled up. Looks like a dashing fellow."

"Dashing and rich," Libby countered. Little Ray flattened his nose against the window and made a face at two passing girls.

"What does he do for a living?" Aaron said.

"Nothing," Libby replied, "absolutely nothing. He just travels and wines and dines himself, considers females a financial liability."

"Well, there is some truth to that," Aaron said. Little Ray glanced at his mom to see her reaction, old enough to recognize the jab. Imagining his grandpa, with his nose pressed against the window, saying females are a financial liability. He giggled to himself. Libby shot him a glare, then redirected it at her father, who quickly changed the subject. "Where is he staying?" Aaron asked.

"He is staying in a suite at the Marriott," Libby replied curtly, reluctant to let the female slander slide but too pleased to be with father and son to let it fester.

"How long does he plan to be in the area?" Aaron asked.

"Who are you?" Libby asked. "Dan Rather? What's with the twenty questions? You haven't asked me a business-related question in six months and all the sudden, you ask twenty"

Little Ray started banging his head against the window, signaling a direction change in the conversation.

"So, Raymond, what are you having for lunch?" Libby asked.

"Grilled cheese," Ray replied.

"We drove all the way into the city for a grilled cheese? I could have made you one of those at home," Aaron said.

"You burn the bread, Grandpa, and your cheese tastes like plastic. We both know we just came here to get Mom out of the office for a little bit." Libby and Aaron looked at each other and smiled. Soon there would be no hiding anything from their young charge, and it warmed their hearts to witness the evolution of their boy/man. As they pulled into the food court, Aaron thought about the Cadillac man. Everything inside him was trying to reason away the dread he felt about the man. He had never made a preemptive strike against someone without any real evidence. For him to do that would require him to become judge and jury, a role he was not sure he would relish. It was way easier to judge a creep who was caught in the act than catch one in the act. He decided he would look into Mr. Evan McGregor's past, find out everything he could about him and keep a very close eye on his activities. He didn't want to alarm Libby, so he decided against involving her just yet.

He put the car in park and made a declaration to Little Ray. "Raymond, I feel so bad about missing our last fishing trip. I promise I will not miss another Saturday fishing trip for the rest of the summer. How bout that"

Ray looked at him suspiciously for a minute, figuring there must be a hitch. Then his face broke into a wide grin as he remembered the words of his mother. "Grandpa Aaron *never* breaks a promise."

CHAPTER 10

Cadillac Man

JAMIE LOOKED AT the list of vehicles Kate had logged during their operation. He had no recollection how he had been transported during his abduction. So every vehicle on the list was a possibility. Any body styles that had two doors or were compact were moved to the bottom of the list with the service and company vehicles. They would be looked at later, much later. First on the list were those designated as suspicious. Kate and he were slowly screening them by finding the title holder and doing a criminal background check on each individual. It was a tedious process and virtually every owner they checked had a record. So they decided to look first at those with a history of domestic violence, stalking, or racial violence. They thought the Gatekeeper might be the skinhead, intolerant type. That list had 123 names on it. *What a neighborhood!* Jamie thought. *Good place to lose a kid or wife.* He thought of the hours Kate had sat alone in her car during the stake-out. It was a miracle she hadn't been approached. He went back to the list. They were also looking for anyone with children, so they could cross-check their offspring with county death records to see if they might have a grieving parent casing the neighborhood.

Aaron pulled the old construction van around behind the Marriot and saw the maroon Cadillac parked in a reserved spot near the door. He backed up next to a dumpster and opened his laptop. He did an ID check on one Evan McGregor, fifty-two years old, born in Berkeley, California, child of Ian and Char McGregor, now deceased. Both were talented software engineers and very wealthy. No known criminal history, no known work history, no negative comments of any kind. He did, however, hold four different driver's licenses in as many different states, each having as many as five speeding tickets against them. The citations were written from the west coast to the east coast. All were paid on time without penalties. Aaron imagined the Cadillac man racing around the country in some kind of a fever, trying to get from Point A to Point B, or maybe he was trying to get away from someone or something. As he pondered the meaning of the many infractions, the man came out and got in his car at 10:30 a.m. *Let's see what a rich, single, spoilt man does with his day,* Aaron said to himself. *Please meet a hot cougar and have lunch somewhere,* Aaron pleaded with the Cadillac man telepathically. He followed the car into traffic, being careful to keep a safe distance and not draw attention to himself. The Cadillac headed west out of town toward the strip malls at a leisurely pace. He was relieved when the Cadillac pulled into a local sports bar. Aaron eased past the establishment, chastening himself for being so paranoid about the man. He continued down the road a half mile and turned around. As he made his way back past the bar, he saw the Cadillac parked in the back lot, facing away from the building. In front of the Cadillac and across the service road was a brightly colored building surrounded by a chain-link fence. The name on the building struck fear in Aaron's heart, Little Light Day Care Center. On cue, children ranging in age from three to seven came streaming out to the playground for their eleven o'clock recess. The man in the Cadillac seemed to sit up straighter and the brake lights fluttered twice.

Aaron's paranoia returned with a vengeance. Threatening to consume him, he tried to steady his breathing. *Think,* he said, *I can't wait for him to hurt someone, and I can't act without serious evidence.* In his heart, Aaron knew. The Cadillac man was a predator unlike any he had dealt with before.

Daryl, the head parts guy at the local GM dealership could not believe it. The richest man in Ann Arbor was standing a mere five feet away and requesting his help. *Unbelievable!* "What can I do for you, Mr. Reynolds?"

"Well, Daryl, I have a situation. I got out of my car at the house and left my keys in the ignition."

"What about you're other set?" Daryl asked.

"They are in my briefcase, in the car. This is really quite embarrassing, Daryl. If we could keep this between us, that would be wonderful."

Daryl thought for a moment. "Your remotes are with your keys, I assume?"

"Yes," Aaron said.

"As you know, Mr. Reynolds, Cadillac keys are very special. They have encoded chips built right into them. It takes two weeks to get a replacement from the company." Aaron couldn't hide his disappointment. "There is, however, a way around that," Daryl said with a sly grin. "If you can get me the VIN number of your car, I can sell you a new remote and use the VIN number to program it to your vehicle. All you have to do then is hit your power lock button, open the door, and retrieve your keys."

"Wonderful!" Aaron exclaimed. "I have some appointments this afternoon. But I'll be in tomorrow about this time. Can we do it then?" Aaron asked.

"No problem, Mr. Reynolds. I'd be glad to help."

"Great! And Daryl, this is our secret, right? Maybe I can help you sometime. Libby's always looking for capable young people, if you ever consider getting out of the automotive field."

Daryl's jaw fell visibly slack, and Aaron was pleased with the affect his offer had on the young salesman.

"Tomorrow then"

"Yes, sir, Mr. Reynolds," Daryl said, resisting the urge to call him "boss." As Aaron left, Daryl pictured his feet crossed on a cherry desk, getting coffee from a beautiful secretary. He had never been much for keeping secrets, but this one was going in the vault for sure.

The next day, Aaron arrived at the Marriot at 8:00 a.m. After booking a room, he strolled down the long corridor that led to the back parking lot. He stepped out the back door and stretched. The maroon Cadillac was parked in its reserved parking spot. He took out his cell phone and pretended to make a call. As he finished his fictitious call, he looked in the window to admire the luxury car's interior, quickly and discretely snapping a photo of the car's VIN number through the windshield.

Sixteen hours later, after acquiring a remote from Daryl and having it programmed to the vin number he had photographed, Aaron pulled the old van around behind the Marriot and parked in the shadows of the adjoining building. The time was 2:00 a.m. and all was quiet in the downtown area. His heart was racing. He was taking a terrible chance doing what he was about to do, but he had to know. He had to confirm his suspicions about Evan McGregor. He reached in his pocket and retrieved the remote. He pulled his ball cap down over his eyes and opened the door of the van. The damp morning air chilled his bones and cooled his brow. He reached in his pocket and felt for his room key. He slowly walked toward the Cadillac, trying to be one with the night, neither threatening nor vulnerable. He paused when he reached the back of the car, looked around once, and hit the trunk button on the remote. The car responded with a satisfying click. He quickly opened the lid and bent to his task. A briefcase and a nylon duffel bag were all it contained. Aaron didn't know exactly what he was looking for, but this sparse inventory was oddly ominous. He tried the latch on the briefcase. Locked. He quickly unzipped the duffel bag and made a mental note of the contents: a Polaroid camera, a length of rope, two rolls of duct tape, four pairs of jersey gloves, and a large survival knife. Aaron knew what he was looking at, a rape kit! He closed the trunk just as the rear door of the motel opened.

There under the rear light of the Marriott stood Evan McGregor. *Did he see me in the trunk?* Aaron asked himself as he put his hand on the corner of the Cadillac and bent over, faking a bout of the dry heaves. He stood up and stared at the back door of the Marriott, ignoring the quiet stranger standing under the security light. Looking like a drunk surveying the last twenty yards to his destination and considering his odds of success, slowly Aaron staggered toward the door as he fished in multiple pockets for his entry card. He finally found it and held it up for the stranger to see. "Bingo," he said, sounding quite pleased with himself.

Evan stepped aside as he passed and followed Aaron to the door with his eyes. Aaron felt the hard glare on his back as he opened the door on his third try. He did not look back to see if his ruse had worked. He was sure a backward glance would negate his drunken performance.

"Captain Wells wants to see us asap, Kate!" Jamie said. "Grab something to write on. I'll meet you upstairs in five."

"What about?" Kate mouthed.

"I have no idea, but he seemed more stressed than usual."

As Kate grabbed her pen and pad, she wondered if Captain Wells had heard the scoop on her and Jamie. It was tough working in a building full of detectives. Secrets were almost impossible to keep. Kate arrived just as Jamie was walking in.

"Close the door, Kate," Captain Wells said. "Sit down, you guys. I've just been informed by the FBI that the body of a boy from Lincoln, Nebraska, was found west of the city this morning. They are getting involved because the boy was transported across state lines. They believe we might have a serial child murderer in our state. Just last week, we had another abduction in Saline, a young boy. He has not been located yet. The FBI thinks it will be just a matter of time before we find his body. They are developing a profile as we speak. And they are very hush-hush about the MO. Listen, I know I have you on this Gatekeeper thing full-time, but I want you both to work with their agents on this We need to get this guy. He's a bad one, bad as they come! They think he could be responsible for as many as two dozen homicides. That's what they are hinting unofficially, anyway. No one wants to stick their neck out, because the numbers are so unbelievable it might cause panic in the suburbs. The only lead they have is a late model maroon luxury car of some kind was seen heading in the direction of the park where the young boy from Saline went missing. Not much to go on. But we should have that profile soon, and that could narrow things down a bit."

Changing the subject, Captain Wells asked Jamie how he was recovering from his ordeal.

"I'm doing good," Jamie said. "It's all kind of like a dream. It's almost hard to believe it even happened. As I look back on it, I don't even think it occurred to Kate and me that an abduction was possible. We were just looking for an angle to get some leads. Tell me about this guy, this Gatekeeper. Is he a nutcase?" Captain Wells asked.

Jamie thought for a moment. "No, he's far from a nut case. Have you ever played chess with someone really good or poker, and at some point in the game, you realize your opponent is always three moves ahead of you? That's how I felt. It was like we were on two different levels."

Captain Wells smiled. "Well, we both know you ain't the sharpest knife in the drawer."

Kate almost said something in defense of her new man, but decided against it. Jamie needed no defending.

"Don't forget, Captain, I was drugged. I was hallucinating and suffocating. It's hard to be sharp under those circumstances. I'm just saying that, after years of dealing with criminals and cops on both sides of the fence, this guy is as smart as they come. He's very confident and capable. He will be hard to catch."

Captain Wells took out a handkerchief and mopped his brow. "So what we have here is a serial child murderer, the likes of which we've never seen before, and a highly intelligent pedophile killer. Too bad we can't get these two together. Save the state a lot of money and manpower."

"We probably have the Gatekeeper's license plate in our notes already," Kate explained. "He had to have been in the neighborhood before he abducted Jamie. It's just a matter of good solid police work. We have to connect the dots, research the owners of the rest of these vehicles, and check their backgrounds. Another week and we should have some solid leads."

"I hope so!" Captain Wells said. "Oh! Another thing! I want you to get Zelda on board. I know you don't like her, Jamie," he said, "but she's been helpful in the past, and I'd like you to let her look at what you got. Try and keep an open mind." He took his coat off the back of his chair, signaling an end to their impromptu meeting. "Now get out there. I pay you two to beat the streets and catch bad guys. This ain't Captain Wells's love boat," he said as he charged off down the hall.

Jamie looked at Kate. She shrugged her shoulders and smiled. "I do not kiss and tell."

Jamie thought for a moment. He hadn't said a word to anybody. He did, however, feel like he had a big sign written across his forehead that said: "I've got the hots for Kate!"

Cadillac Man

Evan McGregor considered the man in the parking lot as he made his late-night run to the party store for cigars. *Something about him seemed off. He didn't look like a drunk and he didn't act like a drunk. He seemed more like an actor in a B movie, exaggerating his words and movements, pretending to be drunk. But why would he pretend to be drunk at 2:00 a.m.? And why had he been leaning against the rear of the Cadillac?* Evan pulled into the late night store and got out of the car. He went to the rear and opened the trunk. Everything appeared as he had left it, almost! He picked up the duffel bag and inspected it. The zipper was open about four inches. He tried to remember the last time he had closed it, when he left the park in Saline. Memories of that evening came back to him, the smell of dirt and the green scent of moss and leaves, the tangy iron smell of blood and fear. He had been quite excited when he left. He could easily have forgotten to close the bag completely. The exciting recollection and the plausible explanation for the open zipper eased his concerns about the drunken man at the Marriott. He went inside and purchased two bottles of their best Merlot and a handful of their finest cigars. He thought he'd go down to the river in the morning and see if the boys were fishing. He had the rest of the summer to fulfill his fantasy, one that involved multiple young fawns . . .

CHAPTER 11

The River Road

LITTLE RAY SAT with his back to the sun, enjoying the warmth on his shoulders as he watched his bobber bouncing on the slight chop of the blue-green river. Something had been nibbling away at his bait for the last ten minutes, refusing to commit to a hard strike. Suddenly, his bobber disappeared beneath the surface. Ray pulled hard. "Missed him. Dang it!" Ray growled.

"Well, looks like this spot cooled off," his friend said.

"Yeah, probably just a turtle messing with my worm."

"You wanna try my spot?" the man asked.

Ray looked at him for a moment. "You say there's lots of fish?"

"Sure is. I've never went there and not caught any."

"Might as well give it a try," Ray said.

"Grab your gear," the man said. "The sooner we get there, the sooner we can start catching fish."

The two started up the hill toward the shiny Cadillac.

Aaron woke with a start, covered in sweat. The dream had been so real . . . his jaw hurt from clenching his teeth. His heart was still racing when the phone rang. "Hello?" he answered on the second ring.

"Hello, handsome. How's my best buddy doing this morning? You sound kind of out of breath."

"No, I'm good. Just had to scramble for the phone. How are you, Susan?" Aaron inquired.

"Fine, just wondering if I could get you to take me on a date for lunch . . . My sister called and wondered if we could join her and James at a fund-raiser she's co-sponsoring on Saturday. I told her I could talk you into almost anything . . . What do you say?"

"I can't!" Aaron said curtly. "I have to take Little Ray fishing. I promised him."

"Aaron, you and Little Ray have been fishing every Saturday all summer long. Can't you take him on Sunday?"

"No," Aaron said without hesitating. "Saturday is our day."

"Can't he go with his buddies this Saturday? . . . If you do this for me, I'll . . ."

"*No*, Susan, I can't. I have to watch out for Raymond!"

"Well, you do what you have to do . . . I'll go to the fund-raiser by myself. Good-bye, Aaron," she said and hung up the phone.

Aaron sat for a long time with the phone in his lap . . . This business with Evan McGregor was taking its toll on him . . . Everyone around him was suffering because of the tension and fear that seemed to grip him since the night he discovered the contents in Evan's trunk. He wished he could just go to the police with his information, but doing so would compromise his other endeavors. The next day, he would wait at the coffee shop and see if the Cadillac man stopped there for breakfast again, then follow him and see if he went out to the park by the river. The more he could learn about his comings and goings, the better. Soon, Aaron knew he would have to act. If a child was killed because he had been indecisive, he would not be able to live with himself.

Kate put the strobe on the dash as Jamie maneuvered the unmarked through the south-bound traffic on Route 27. They had just received a radio dispatch from Captain Wells. The body of a young boy had been found . . . at the park in Saline, Michigan. The crime scene had been secured, and they were waiting for Jamie and Kate to arrive before processing the body. Captain Wells was already at the scene along with Special Agent Richard Martinez with the FBI.

If the small town was aware of the tragedy unfolding at the park, it didn't show as they drove through town. People seemed to be going about their daily chores, getting mail, groceries, and gas. They continued east out of town.

At the park, the scene was different; two squad cars, lights flashing, sat blocking the entrance to the park. Jamie flashed his credentials and eased through the road block . . . The sky was overcast and the lack of sunlight caused the giant oaks that lined the drive into the park to cast pale sinister shadows across the Kentucky bluegrass that carpeted the interior of the park. As they made their way deeper into the park, Kate tried to survey the scene from the perpetrator's prospective . . . *Had he come to kill?* she thought . . . *Or was this a crime of opportunity?* With only one way in and out of the park, she felt the man had been desperate to kill . . . Why else would he risk spending time with his victim in this public place?

They reached the end of the paved parkway and continued on following the tracks left in the grass by the multitude of vehicles that had preceded them. Soon they saw a flurry of activity at the north-east end of the park. Plain-clothed officers and techs dug through open car trunks for equipment and clipboards. Jamie caught a glimpse of two techs disappearing into the undergrowth, hands full of equipment, as an ashen-faced detective emerged from the same trail . . . Jamie parked the car . . . He watched the man walk to the back of a cruiser and lean over the side. The man seemed to be sobbing . . . his shoulders bouncing up and down. Jamie sat with his hands on the wheel watching him . . . wondering if the man was weak . . . or if the scene was really bad . . . His answer came when the man turned slightly and gave one last great heave, expelling the last of his stomachs contents into the bushes beside the cruiser. "Why do we do this shit, Katie?" he said.

She didn't answer him . . . but continued to watch the detective . . . as he mopped his forehead and mouth with a kerchief . . . He looked around to see if his moment of weakness had been witnessed. Jamie and Kate averted their eyes as his gaze turned to them. They both got out of the car and went to the trunk. They leaned in and retrieved two pairs of rubber gloves, a notepad, and a small tape recorder.

"Are you ready for this, doll?" he said.

"It's what we get paid for. Let's do it."

Jamie turned the recorder on and said, "This is Detective James Larson. The date is 6 November 2010, time 2:14 p.m. I am accompanied by Detective Kate Wagner. We are at the Saline, Michigan, Memorial Park investigating the homicide of a young boy . . . stand by. Jamie clicked off the recorder and motioned for Kate to follow. They followed a beaten path about a quarter mile back into the densest part of the park. It seemed to be a deer trail that had been there for many years, borrowed occasionally by adventurous teenagers and hikers. The farther they went, the darker it seemed to get. The hardwoods overhead created a dense, almost rainforest-like canopy. The smell of decaying human remains assaulted their noses as the trail abruptly opened into a small clearing, where Captain Wells and a distinguished-looking, steel-eyed detective stood talking quietly.

"Jamie . . . Kate . . . this is Special Agent Richard Martinez . . . with the FBI. Have a look at the body, then meet us at my car. Agent Martinez has that profile for you straight from Quantico, and he'd like to get your take on what you find here . . . See you in a bit . . . I can't take this smell another minute. With that, they turned and left Kate and Jamie alone in the clearing. Kate walked carefully up to the body, which was covered with a plastic tarp to discourage the flies and gnats that seemed to fill the air.

Jamie clicked on the recorder as Kate slowly pulled back the plastic tarp. The first noise he recorded was an audible gasp by Kate. A young boy lay on his stomach, his head turned at an impossible angle. His face was a mummified death mask without eyes. After three weeks in the Michigan summer, scavengers had claimed the softest parts of the body. Jamie spoke in the recorder, "Subject is a male Caucasian, approximately eight years old. Body is in the late stages of decomposition. It is completely nude except for socks . . . ribs are partially visible due to carnivore scavenging. Visible knife wounds can be seen in the back and neck area . . . The victim's mouth is filled with leaves and dirt." . . . Jamie remembered a class he had taken on serial rapists. The most infamous being Andre Chikatilo, the sadistic Russian killer responsible for the rape and murder of dozens of women and children . . . His MO was to stuff his victims' mouths with whatever was at hand, usually dirt and leaves . . . Jamie continued, "It appears that a hasty attempt to decapitate the victim was unsuccessful, as the scull is still attached by one thick tendon." Jamie looked at Kate . . . A lone tear had made its way down her face and hung stubbornly from her chin, refusing to let go. "It appears that the homicide took place where the body lies, as blood has saturated and stained the ground beneath the body." Jamie turned the recorder off . . . Kate looked around the area . . . One tennis shoe hung from a fork in a small sapling . . . A dirty, worn T-shirt lay washed flat to the ground by numerous rainfalls. A small pair of trousers lay in a pile near the body. Kate picked them up with a gloved hand, examining them carefully.

Two crime scene techs broke the silence. "Is it OK if we start baggin' and taggin' . . . ?"

"Yes, of course," Jamie said. "I want pics before and after you turn the body over, and of each garment before you bag it, please."

"No problem. We'll handle it," the tech said.

With that, Jamie led the way out of the clearing. As they made their way down the trail, Kate seemed to lag behind. Jamie slowed on two occasions and was about to chastise Kate for being so slow, when she stopped and got down on all fours. Before he could ask her what was up, she was climbing into the impenetrable thicket . . . She soon backed her way out, pulling something behind her . . . She laid her prize on the trail at Jamie's feet, a radio-controlled off-road truck complete with duct-tape repairs sat squashed like an annoying cockroach . . . with one perfect, muddy shoe-print on the center of its roof. The tread pattern looked like that of a high-end loafer or boat shoe . . .

Detective Martinez was waiting for them when they came out. Captain Wells had decided to call it a day. He handed Jamie a manila envelope. "This is a copy of the killer's profile generated by Quantico. Look it over and give me a call if you have any questions. So!" he said . . ."How do you think it went down?"

Jamie looked at Kate. "I believe it was a crime of opportunity," she said. "I think our guy considered what he was about to do, weighed the risks, and acted . . . I believe he is a sexual sadist . . . I think he was frustrated and would have liked to spend more time with his victim . . . I believe he will kill again. It's just a matter of time."

Detective Martinez considered her assessment for a moment. "You say he considered the risk and acted . . . How so?"

"Well," Kate said, "the boy's clothes were well worn . . . holes in the jeans and shirt, one sneaker had a hole worn in the bottom. Our guy watched him until there were no witnesses. He probably figured by the boy's dress that his parents were probably working, lower class, and unlikely to look for him until he had been missing for a few hours."

"Very good," the FBI agent said. "Why do you think he was frustrated?"

"Because one shoe was found in the fork of a tree, indicating a violent initial attack . . . and his attempt to decapitate the victim. Also this . . ." Kate sat the box containing the smashed toy truck down on the ground . . . "We have a perfect, frustrated shoe-print."

Aaron arrived at the coffee shop about 8:30. He went inside and sat in a booth at the far end. He was about to leave when he saw the Cadillac pull into a parking spot in the front. Evan McGregor strolled in with the confidence of a DC politician. He asked the attendant for a latte and a muffin, made small talk with another person in line, then casually made his way toward the door. His hand was on the handle of the door when something caught his eye and seemed to freeze him in place. He reached in his pocket for coins and inserted them into a newspaper vending machine. The lid opened and he took out a copy of the local newspaper. He stared transfixed at the front page for a long time, then exited the shop. He looked nervously around, tore the front page off, and discarded the rest of the paper in the waste can near the door. He looked at the paper remnant once more, folded it, and put it in his jacket pocket. He got in the Cadillac and eased out of the parking lot toward Riverside Park. Aaron quickly made his way towards the door as he fished for coins . . . After grabbing a copy of the same paper, he got in his pickup and followed the Cadillac out towards the park. Aaron could see the maroon car approaching the entrance to the park . . . it slowed but did not turn in. Aaron also slowed, not wanting to overtake the driver of the Cadillac, who seemed lost in thought and unsure of his destination. The Cadillac continued for a half mile, crossing the river bridge. Aaron was about to turn off and return to town, content to have the man out of the city, when the Cadillac stopped at the entrance to the old river road. The driver seemed to be contemplating something. Aaron could not help but overtake his quarry. He pulled up behind the man who was looking down the river road, oblivious to the pickup truck behind him . . . Aaron honked his horn and the man seemed to snap out of his trance . . . He looked once in the rearview mirror, then turned quickly on to the old dead end road. Aaron continued on past as he watched the Cadillac disappear from sight down the old road.

Maybe he's trying to shake me off his tail, Aaron thought. To follow him down that road would have been a dead giveaway. Aaron continued out of town for a few miles, then turned off on a county road. He pulled his truck to the shoulder and put it in park. He unfolded the paper he had purchased . . . The headline on the front page read: "Body of Saline Boy is Found." The article went on to say the FBI was now involved and had issued a profile of the killer. Police had no suspects, but a late model, maroon luxury car was seen in the vicinity of the park where the body was found, and the driver was considered a person of interest. A hotline had been set up for any information about the crime or the vehicle. Anonymous callers were to ask for Detective Kate Wagner.

Aaron reached in his glove box and retrieved a track phone he had purchased with cash for just such an occasion.

He dialed the number of the hotline. Kate took the call from dispatch.

"This is Detective Wagner. Who am I speaking to . . . ?"

The line was quiet for a moment. Then a voice said, "I am the Gatekeeper . . . Tell Detective Larson the maroon luxury car he is looking for is registered to an Evan McGregor and has California plate number JLY 5674. Tell him if he does not address this situation in a prompt, decisive manner, I *will*. He will know what I mean."

With that, the line went dead. Jamie looked at Kate, waiting for an explanation for the shocked look on her face . . . "It was him," she said.

"Him who?" Jamie asked.

"The Gatekeeper. He told me to give you this number . . . He said if you don't address the situation, he will."

Jamie stared at the paper for a moment, then picked up the phone. "Get me the BMV," he said to the dispatcher. As he waited to be transferred, he held his hand over the receiver,. "Kate, get online. Find out anything you can about California resident Evan McGregor, birth records, pay stubs, financial records, addresses, tax returns. I wanna know where he lives, where he works, what he drives. I want everything. We need to find this guy before Robin Hood does."

CHAPTER 12

The Profile

As KATE SEARCHED for Evan McGregor's information, Jamie opened the manila envelope Detective Martinez had given him and began to read the profile: "Suspect is believed to be a Caucasian male, aged thirty-five to forty-five years old . . . highly intelligent with ample resources . . . It is believed that he is acting alone . . . and unlikely to share knowledge of his crime with a confidant because of extreme antisocial tendencies . . . He will likely kill until he is caught and is believed to be responsible for at least a dozen child homicides. He is a pedophile in the classic sense of the word, preferring males to females." Jamie sat the file aside and picked up the list Kate had been working on . . . She had whittled down the list of vehicle plates they had collected on their sting to just a few . . . an exterminator . . . called Ex-term and a construction van with company name R&D Construction. He punched the Ex-term plate into the BMV computer and started looking for the owner . . . Apparently Ex-term was a franchise owned by a small company in town . . . He got a phone number and called to see who might have been driving the vehicle on the date in question. The clerk on the other end of the line seemed unwilling to offer any information that might help the investigation, choosing rather to be vague about times, dates, and employees. Jamie suspected that they were probably paying their help in cash and did not want to attract the attention of the IRS. He finally tired of her stonewalling and informed her that hindering a homicide investigation was a felony. She quickly gave him the information he needed and the name of the employee that was working in the neighborhood that day. Jamie thanked her for her time and did a criminal history check on the employee in question. He came up clean . . . only a few traffic tickets and considering his age, twenty-two, he was unlikely to have children old enough to have fallen victim to foul play. Jamie quickly ruled him out as a suspect.

Next up, Jamie punched in the number of the old construction van. It was registered to a company called

R&D Construction that had split up over fifteen years ago. The title had ended up in probate when the assets were split up. The vehicle had not been retitled since . . . Jamie probed a little further and found that R&D stood for Reynolds and Dominique. He sat back in his chair and considered his findings . . . Why would somebody be driving around a van that had not been titled in fifteen years, with a current plate on it? Kate leant across his desk, being careful to flash a sufficient amount of cleavage to command immediate attention. The visual stimuli coupled with the scent of her sandalwood body lotion caused Jamie to sit up straight and flash her a million-dollar smile. "Any luck?" he said, forgetting about the old van plate.

"Well," she said, "it appears that Evan McGregor is very wealthy. His tax return last year was fifty-four pages long. He has money he doesn't even know about!"

"So where is he?" Jamie asked.

"Can't say for sure. He's been traveling most of his adult life, never stays in one place longer than a year or so. Next step is to check bank records, see if I can get a credit card number. Maybe we can track his movements with credit receipts. Gonna take a warrant, though. Should I call Captain Wells and get it started?"

"Absolutely, and throw him a bone. Tell him we're on our way to see the Great Zelda!"

Kate relayed the info to Captain Wells as they made their way out of town toward the home of the renowned psychic, Zelda Jimenez.

"God! This lady gives me the creeps," Jamie said, "can't even speak English. How can you live most of your life in the good old USA and not speak English?"

Kate chose not to criticize the old woman, in case she really could read minds. "She's a sweet old woman," she said as they pulled into the driveway of a large, old, Victorian three-story painted a vivid lavender color. The sign out front said: "Zelda 'Spiritual Guide,' Know Your Future, Visit Your Past." Kate grabbed the file and led the way to the front door as Jamie looked around nervously, hoping that no one would see him going into the big pink clown house. A middle-aged man named Felix introduced himself as Zelda's son. He led them into a large parlor of sorts, where all three sat on one side of a large oak table that was skirted in burgundy velour. The walls and window panes were painted a deep burgundy color. Light filtered through the brush strokes on the glass, creating the appearance of two large, square, bloodshot eyes. The velour-tasseled valances completed the illusion by adding eyebrows. Jamie shifted uneasily in his chair; he glanced at Felix, who was sitting quietly, head bowed. He looked at Kate and shrugged his shoulders; Kate gave him a scolding look and bowed her own head.

Before he could decide what to do with his head, an ancient figure materialized in the arched doorway that led from the other room. Her face was veiled with a black lace material of some kind, and she wore a burgundy full-length robe wrapped tightly around what Jamie guessed to be a ninety-pound frame. She spoke what sounded like one word in Spanish, causing Felix to welcome them on behalf of his mother and ask how the humble Zelda might be of assistance. Kate produced photos of the crime scene in Saline. She laid them on the table in front of Zelda, and then she sat pictures of the Gatekeeper's victims beside those. Zelda put her hand on the photo of the murdered boy from Saline. She closed her eyes and began to mumble quietly in what sounded like an ancient Portuguese dialect of some kind. Suddenly, her eyes snapped open and she began to shake uncontrollably (she spoke the odd language for sometime as Felix listened closely). As quickly as she started, she stopped and looked at Felix with great concern.

"My mother says a bastard did this, a fatherless son, who had no guidance from a human father. She says his father is a demon spirit. She says he has an evil heart, a very dark heart."

"Amazing!" Jamie said to Kate. "Our killer is a mean bastard with an evil heart! Wouldn't have figured that!" He turned to Felix. "Tell your mother we kinda figured that! Ask her if she can tell us something we don't know!"

Felix relayed the message to his mother, who looked long and hard at Jamie before placing her hand on the photos of the Gatekeeper's victims one at a time. She closed her eyes and with a calm smile, said one word in broken English, "Oppositeo . . ."

Jamie looked at Felix, intrigued by her one word response. "What's that mean," he urged?

Felix seemed to consider his question for a moment, then said, "The killer of these men is different than the killer of the boy . . . He is the opposite."

Jamie, exasperated with the whole experience, stood to leave. Before Jamie could make a scene, Kate asked Felix what he thought that meant.

Felix cleared his throat and began to render his interpretation. "The man who killed the boy was a fatherless son with an evil heart. The man who killed these others is a sonless father with a good heart!"

Libby Reynolds cradled the phone against her neck as she put a handful of spaghetti noodles in the scalding pan of water. "I know, Susan. I've noticed too. He seems very tense lately. I know he adores you. Please don't read too much into his actions. He and Ray have been spending a lot of time together lately. Maybe it's time for a break. Tell you what, Susan. Let me pull a few strings and see if I can't get him to join us for your luncheon.

Raymond and I would love to come, and we'll all get a chance to see Dad and help raise some capital for your charity."

"Libby, that would be wonderful! Make sure you're not too obvious. I don't want Aaron to think he's being coerced into joining us."

"No problem," Libby said, "let me handle it." They exchanged goodbyes and Libby finished preparing supper as she pondered her next move.

Little Ray and his father ate like they were starving, consuming all the spaghetti, meatballs, and most of the garlic bread. Little Ray looked up from his plate and smiled. One long noodle hung from his chin. As it disappeared with one last slurp, Lilly was struck by the display. How many times had she seen her brother Aaron Jr do the same thing and how similar the two looked at this age! Aaron Jr had been nine years old when he was murdered, and Ray Jr would be nine years old in two weeks. A sudden gust of cool summer air slammed the front door shut with a loud thump. With a jolt, she looked up to find herself alone at the table. The boys had retired to the den and left her alone with her thoughts. Her heartbeat slowly began to steady. But the memory of her brother and his resemblance to her son lingered in her subconscious. A feeling of dread tried to grip her. She walked through the kitchen and looked into the den, needing a visual of her son before she could dismiss the unwelcome foreboding. She returned to the kitchen and picked up the phone. She hit number one on the speed dial and waited for her father to answer.

"Hey, Dad, how is everything?"

"Great!" Aaron replied enthusiastically, throwing her slightly off balance as she considered what to say next.

"Listen, Dad, I just talked to Susan about her fund-raiser this Saturday. She'd like Raymond, myself, and you to join her."

Aaron interrupted, "I know. I talked to her yesterday. I told her Little Ray and I would be fishing. I don't think she was pleased."

"Dad, that's why I'm calling. Little Ray has Little League tryouts this Saturday, so I thought rather than going fishing by yourself, you could come with us to the fund-raiser. Susan would really like you to come."

Aaron seemed to be processing this new information, and Libby waited quietly for his response . . . "Well," he said, "if Ray's gonna be busy, sure I'd love to join you guys."

"Great!" Libby said. "Can I tell Susan you'll pick her up at 11:00 a.m.?"

"Absolutely," Aaron replied. Aaron hung up the phone thankful for this turn of events that would allow him to make up to Susan for his rude behavior. She would be a pleasant distraction during the trying time. And spending time with Libby was always a joy. Raymond's conversations tended to be a little one-dimensional, but he could listen to his son-in-law and feign interest for an hour or so.

Cadillac Man

The man sat overlooking the city from his balcony on the top floor of the Marriott . . . pondering the events of the past few weeks. He was not accustomed to being cautious. He was Evan McGregor, the son of Ian and Char McGregor, above suspicion. He was privileged, always had been. Only once, in all these years of seeking the companionship of the innocent, had he ever been caught in the act. It had been a humiliating experience; the thought of it caused him pain. He sat staring at the smoldering cigar in the ashtray. The cherry-flavored smoke danced on the breeze, teasing his nostrils, bringing with it memories of long ago, a different time, a time when he was awkward and undeveloped, a time of learning, about himself and what he was becoming, always trying to understand why he felt cold inside and violent. Other people would look at a young child, a puppy, or a kitten and want to hold it and caress it. Evan wanted to choke it and crush the life out of it, slowly, because once the life was gone, no more satisfaction could be had. It had taken him time to learn to be patient and get the maximum enjoyment out of each encounter. The acrid cherry smoke filled his head now, slowly peeling back layers of insulation, carefully and painfully applied to memories long forgotten. It reminded him of his father, all smug, sitting in his leather recliner, puffing away on a Cuban, telling Evan how privileged he was and how grateful he should be for having such intelligent and worldly parents. Later, as Evan struggled to make grades at the university, his father harassed him constantly about his work ethics, about his lack of female companionship, and his grades. The final straw came one weekend when Evan was home on spring break.

He had coaxed the neighbor boy up to the guest room of their big house after enjoying a dip in the pool, thinking his parents were away for the evening. He would have killed for the first time, if his father had not stormed in and pulled the young boy free. His father had taken the boy downstairs, brushed him off, and looked him over. After seeing no visible signs of injury, he offered the boy a Coke and slipped him three, crisp, hundred-dollar bills. He told him if he could keep the incident a secret, he could come back next week and get three more. The boy agreed and left feeling he had won the lottery. He had in a sense; Lady Luck had spared his young life. No one else would ever again be pulled from his grasp and spared his wrath.

Ian had come upstairs and called him every vile name he could muster from his ample vocabulary. Evan had hoped his father would beat him physically, but Ian, ever the intellectual, was above violence. He chose rather to insult and condemn, meting out punishment verbally and mentally. When it came time to return to school on Sunday evening, Evan's mind was made up. He was twenty years old and no longer needed parents. As he drove out of town toward the USC campus, he stopped in a very rough neighborhood in south Berkeley, where he had bought acid many times before. He found a man he had bought drugs from in the past standing on the same corner as always, meeting the supply and demand of the local college students. He told the man if he would give him thirty hits of acid, he would tell him where he could find $30,000 in cash in a safe. He told him where the safe was and that the couple would be home Monday night and that they had no firearms, so it would be an easy score. Furthermore, he told the dealer that the man of the house was a racist and despised black people. The dealer agreed to the transaction with malicious glee as Evan handed him the address of his mother and father.

Tuesday morning, he was pulled out of class . . . The school chaplain and a sheriff's deputy were waiting in the office. Evan walked in quietly and sat down. The chaplain informed him that his parents had been brutally murdered the evening before. Apparently, robbery had been the motive. Evan buried his face in his hands and tried desperately to cry . . . Unable to shed a single tear, he chose to act shocked into an almost catatonic state . . . his spirit crushed . . . his beloved parents dead . . . he was unable to speak for almost two weeks. This turned out to be a brilliant rouse . . . as he stood quietly in front of his parents' caskets and let his uncle and aunts accept all condolences.

Poor Evan was so devastated he was unable to continue his schooling and chose to get away from the bad memories by traveling abroad for two years, occasionally sending postcards to friends and relatives. When he finally returned to the United States, he began his reign of destruction. Playing the part of a sophisticated playboy . . . aloof and untouchable . . . he intimidated men and left woman fantasizing in his wake. He moved with ease from city to city . . . state to state, always hunting, always hurting, always successful, until now. He looked down at his cigar. It no longer smoldered, the cherry smell no longer lingered, and the pain of the past began to fade. He looked up at the sky, a dark squall line cut a perfect horizontal line across the city's western vista. The air seemed electric, and the warm breeze stopped momentarily, then resumed in cool bursts that seemed to march forward, then retreat. Evan stood and put his hands on the railing. Something was coming; he could feel it! He fought the urge to flee to the sanctuary of his room. He could not run. Lions don't run in the face of a storm. Rather, they choose to hunt and feed using nature's chaos to confuse their prey. The rain came in great horizontal sheets, drenching him completely. Still he stood and faced the storm, not willing to retreat until he had gathered his thoughts. The police were looking for a maroon luxury car in connection to the murder of the dirty boy from Saline. That's all they had. *Maybe it was time for a new car?* He turned from the railing and went inside. He picked up the phone and dialed the concierge. He spoke with practiced authority, "This is Mr. McGregor, Room 1501. Please contact the local Cadillac dealer for me. Tell them I'll be dropping buy to pick up a new car. Tell them there's no need for financing. I'll pay in full with a bank check. Oh, and tell them I have a trade-in." He hung up the phone and smiled to himself as he went to the bathroom to towel off and change. Easy fix for a man of his means.

CHAPTER 13

The Hunted

THE QUIET CHUG of the coffee maker was the only sound in the room. The smell of leather mingling with the scent of the imported Columbian coffee created an aroma that seemed to say, "All is well." The overstuffed leather couch creaked as Evan adjusted his weight to gaze out the tinted window.

Outside, the scene was much more chaotic. A great lion stood motionless, gazing at the crowds of people that thronged across the open lot in front of him. His mouth was open wide, lips curled back in a menacing grin, revealing massive canines. Slowly, he lowered his head until he was close enough to pounce on an unsuspecting family. At the last second, the mother looked up and shrieked with surprise! Her husband and young son doubled over and laughed hysterically as the wind caught the great beast and stood him back up straight. Just then, the PA system squealed, and a voice proclaimed, "Welcome to Matter Horn GM-Cadillac . . . *we're making grrrreat deals* on all GM models, new and used." On cue, the wind came up and the great inflatable beast bent over to attack another family about to investigate a used minivan. Everyone seemed pleased with the side show but the salesman, who looked more like a kindergarten teacher trying to get the attention of an unruly class.

As Evan watched the salesmen scurrying about the lot, clipboards in hand, trying desperately to sell overpriced cars to underfunded customers, a sneer formed on his unlined face. *How pathetic they are, so desperate to make a sale! Like male peacocks spreading their plumes and doing their desperate mating dance, abandoning all dignity to acquire the prize.* He was sure he would never abandon his dignity at any price.

The door opened and Evan's personal peacock entered the VIP waiting room at Matter Horn Cadillac. He was all puffed up, his face flush with success. "Well, Mr. McGregor, I have the keys to your new Escalade. It is completely detailed and ready for you. I must say it's been a privilege doing business with you. And we look forward to serving you in the future."

As Evan took the keys to his new car, he couldn't help but feel invisible again, anonymous. The police were looking for a maroon luxury car, and he was the proud owner of a new black SUV. *Wonderful!* he thought. As the salesman continued gushing about service and brand loyalty, Evan's mind wandered to the dark river and his unfinished business there. Now he could continue his hunt inconspicuously. The salesman continued chattering about warranties and service agreements, as Evan slipped deeper into his lustful fantasy . . . a fantasy that abruptly dissolved as Evan's subconscious replayed something the salesman had just said. "What did you say?" he asked.

The salesman stopped mid-sentence . . . "About what, Mr. McGregor?"

"About your service database."

"Oh, I was asking if you would like us to enter your new car into our database, like your other vehicle, so we can inform you of VIP events and upcoming service specials."

Both men felt a sudden change in the air . . .

"My other vehicle is not in your database," Evan declared. "I've never been here before today."

The salesman seemed to shrink measurably in stature . . . His brightly colored plume seemed to fade . . . "I beg to differ, Mr. McGregor. Only a month ago, you made a purchase from our parts department . . . Your VIN number must have been used to acquire the correct part. That automatically enters you in our database."

"What . . . did I purchase?" Evan asked slowly, articulating each word.

The shaken salesman gathered himself and bent over his laptop glad to escape Evan's menacing glare. After clicking feverishly for a few minutes, he looked up with a broad grin sure, he had resolved the uncomfortable situation. "Our records show you purchased a new remote for your other vehicle the fifteenth of last month."

Kate and Richard Martinez had spent the better part of the afternoon accessing the FBI's extensive data on known shoe impressions and had determined that the shoe imprint found near the crime scene in Saline was that of a shoe manufactured in Italy, by a company called Botticelli and imported to the United States for sale by exclusive, high-end shoe retailers. The list of retailers was a short one . . . The next step was to find out how many of the stores handled that particular model . . . The tread pattern described by Botticelli as the comfort flex tread was exclusive to three models, and the moderate lug pattern was recommended for light-duty hiking . . . thus eliminating retailers in, say, New York City or Chicago, who might tend to favor shoe models used for pounding pavement or carpet, rather than trails or beaches. While

Kate and the dashing FBI agent sat shoulder to shoulder chatting and navigating the web . . . Jamie researched the child homicides that had occurred in the tri-state area over the last fifteen years, slowly eliminating potential suspects by any means possible . . . creating a manageable list that he and Kate could work on later.

Jamie's mind wandered to their last evening together . . . Kate had invited him over for dinner . . . Afterwards, they had sat on the couch and shared a bottle of wine . . . He had gushed about her culinary skills, and she had laughed at his corny cop jokes . . . He could almost hear her sexy, raspy giggle now . . . Actually, he did hear her sexy, raspy giggle now. He slowly turned around, pretending to look for something in his file box. As he did, he stole a glance at Kate's desk . . . The G-man was patting Kate on the back as she tried to suppress a belly laugh. Jamie's face turned red as Kate and Super Hair broke out in peals of laughter. *Damn the FBI, always pushing the limits of their jurisdiction . . . Who was I kidding, anyhow?* Jamie thought to himself. Until a couple of weeks ago, he had not even considered himself worthy to throw his hat into the ring of possible suitors. Kate was young and beautiful, and he was old and . . . not beautiful. He involuntarily slammed the file drawer closed. The noise seemed to startle Kate and Super Hair. They both looked at him like he had spoiled their moment . . . Jamie shrugged and turned to his desk . . . not before Kate saw the hurt in his eyes. The young FBI agent turned back to Kate just as she excused herself to the ladies' room. He appraised her as she walked away, then turned his gaze to Jamie, who was slamming away on his computer with the same zeal as he had closed his file drawer.

Aaron Reynolds sat on the back deck watching the sun come up. Golden tendrils of light pierced the Michigan pines, coming to rest on the cedar shake siding at the rear of the house, slowly moving their way toward the eaves before splashing the green steel roof with light. Like a painter randomly covering a gray canvas with shades of autumn, gold, and forest green, one by one, the army of lights marched upwards, growing in shape and size until they had covered the house and expelled the last remnants of night.

The light felt good, Aaron thought to himself . . . He had spent too much time in the darkness of the chamber over the last year trying to fill the dark hole in his heart, that bottomless pit that yawned open like a great crevasse so many years ago when he looked down at the body of his dead son. Would he ever fill it? Could it even be measured? A morning cloud drifted lazily across the eastern sky, momentarily cooling the sun and steeling its glory, casting the house in a gray cloak once again. Aaron shuddered momentarily as the cloud passed. The day turned warm and bright once more . . . but the chill in Aaron's heart remained. There would be no filling the void. The best he could hope for was to stand at its edge and hurl bodies into the darkness. Perhaps one day, he would hear one find the bottom. Then and only then would he know its depth and understand the task which lay before him.

Cadillac Man

The printer clicked away for a few seconds, then ejected the invoice . . . "There you go," the salesman said, "one remote for Cadillac VIN number CJ125YN62413OPT21."

Evan examined the document carefully for a moment, then laid it on the counter. "Why is there no bill-to name or address, and who is Daryl?"

The salesman looked at the invoice, then said, "Daryl is the head of our parts department."

"Why is his signature on the bottom of the invoice?" Evan asked.

"I don't know," the salesman said transparently. "Let's ask him." He picked up the phone and dialed Parts . . . "Hello, Daryl, this is Jonathan in Sales. Could you come to the VIP waiting room, please? He'll be here in just a few. Would you like a cup of coffee while we wait?"

Evan ignored him, choosing rather to be alone with his thoughts . . . *Perhaps it was an honest mistake of some kind, a computer error.* He would watch Daryl's reaction to their inquiry and he would know; he always knew . . . People lie for two reasons: fear and greed. And years of dealing with the extraordinarily rich and the people who orbit them like satellites had fine-tuned his sense for greed; it was something tangible, hard to disguise . . . You could see it in the fleshy jowls of an overweight CEO or the hard smile lines of a gold-digging female. Greed was there on the surface if you looked for it. And fear; Evan knew fear . . . When he was a boy, he could look at a dog and make it whine . . . something he perfected as he grew older . . . Often, he would look at a man twice his size until the man broke off eye contact, acknowledging Evan as the alpha male in the room. In the same way, a lack of fear or greed was also a tangible thing, like the open face of a simpleton or the clear eyes of a born-again Christian. If it wasn't there, it wasn't there.

Daryl bounded into the room like a motivational speaker making his entrance on stage . . . happy to have been summoned to the exclusive venue by one of his superiors, salesman of the month, Jonathan Meyers. "What can I do for you, Jonathan?" he asked, casting a glance at the invoice lying on the counter.

Jonathan, clearly annoyed at having to converse with an underling like Daryl, got straight to the point. "Explain this invoice to me." He handed it to Daryl, and together, he and Evan watched Daryl's reaction.

He looked at it for a moment and then handed it back to Jonathan without changing his facial expression one bit. "Looks like an order for a remote."

Jonathan clapped his hands together mockingly. "Wow! You're good," he said sarcastically. "Why is your signature on the invoice? And why does the owner of the car not remember ordering it or ever being in our dealership for that matter?"

Daryl slowly took the invoice from Jonathan again and looked at it closely for a long time. Evan watched him study the document clearly and honestly, trying to decipher its content . . . Then Evan saw what he was looking for . . . The vein on Daryl's temple seemed to twitch, then throb ever so slightly. A light sheen of moisture appeared at his hairline.

The salesman, oblivious to the subtle signals being displayed by Daryl, grew impatient and began using hand gestures again. "Hello! Anybody there?" he said, using his best President Parade wave.

Daryl chanced a glance at Evan and was instantly trapped in his penetrating stare; something passed between them . . . the knowledge of betrayal . . . like Jesus and Judas. Daryl started stuttering about possible transposed numbers in the VIN, while Evan put on his jacket. Without addressing either of them, he picked up the keys to his new car and left the room.

As he pulled away from the dealership, the great inflatable lion growled again, reminding him of the hunt . . . a hunt that just got infinitely more complicated. Perhaps he should just move on to another place, another unsuspecting town. Why did he feel compelled to stay and risk so much? What was the attraction to this place; to these boys? . . . It was like the universe was conspiring against his success here. *Someone was going to great lengths to invade his privacy, to undermine his success, to spoil his hunt!* And somehow, it made him more resolute, more determined, more anxious to have his way. It thrilled him to imagine the failure his unseen adversary would feel as he stood amidst the destruction that Evan would leave behind. Perhaps he would leave him a note, taunt him intellectually, chastise him for his ignorance and his failure to stop the inevitable. Evan felt that great heat in his belly starting to rise, to take control. He fought the urge to give in to the carnality of it. His time would come and he would release his bloodlust. Then he would slip away like a dark shadow into a new night.

CHAPTER 14

The Banquet

THE ROOM WAS already buzzing with activity when Aaron and Susan, accompanied by Libby and Raymond, entered. The decibel level rose noticeably but discreetly as they negotiated their way through the crowd. It was common knowledge that Aaron and his daughter Libby would be present. And that Reynolds & Reynolds Financial was clearly the largest contributor that would be in attendance. But to many in the room, Aaron Reynolds was a cross between Ted Nugent and Donald Trump, a charismatic, rich, home-grown wolverine, and seeing him in person was no small thing. Susan noticed the stir her date was creating and pulled him closer, smiling up at him.

Aaron returned her smile as she led him to a table near the front. Susan's sister greeted them each with a kiss and seated them before making her way to the podium.

"I'd like to thank each and every one of you for taking time from your busy schedules to share this wonderful evening with us, and assure you that every single donation received this evening will go to help victims of violent crime. As you know . . . the negative effects of violent crime continue long after the crime has been committed, whether you are the parent of a murdered child," she said, casting a solemn nod to Aaron, "or the victim of rape or incest, the residual effects can be devastating and often require years of therapy. Our mission is two-fold . . . first . . . to make sure *no one suffers alone!*" Spontaneous applause erupted from the crowd, then slowly faded. "With your help, our counselors are available 24/7, three hundred and sixty-five days a year. And second . . . our goal is to make sure our men and women on the front lines have the proper equipment and leadership needed to perform their duties safely and effectively, making the state of Michigan a safer place to live and raise a family."

Several uniformed police officers stood and clapped their hands vigorously, as the balance of the room stood and joined the applause. While the crowd continued to applaud, the lights dimmed and the MC bounded to the podium. "Please give a warm welcome to Michigan's own,

Columbia recording artist, Sierra Garcia, singing her new hit single 'Love Comes Easy.'"

As the beautiful singer sang about love and the ease with which it came, Aaron held Susan's hand and looked into her eyes. She returned his gaze with a confident smile. He kissed her cheek and she whispered something in his ear. They both smiled and turned their attention back to the stage, where the singer continued her romantic ballad. After singing the chorus for the third and final time, she held her hand out straight and silently mouthed the words "Love Comes Easy." The crowd gave her a standing ovation and the lights came up, revealing a host of servers scurrying about the room with bowls of salad and steaming rolls. The din of conversation rose slowly to a civilized level as people renewed old acquaintances and caught up on local gossip.

The primary topic seemed to be the Gatekeeper and his identity. Aaron heard an inebriated man at the table behind him make a toast to the Gatekeeper. "Let God be the judge, but let the Gatekeeper arrange the meeting. To the Gatekeeper!" he proclaimed, raising his glass.

Aaron lifted his glass in turn and looked around the room . . . *For justice!* he thought to himself as he took a drink of dark red wine.

Jamie decided to do a little Saturday afternoon detective work. Kate had said something about a baby shower and that she would be off the radar for the better part of the afternoon, and Detective Martinez was noticeably absent. So Jamie did what he always did when he was pissed at a female . . . he worked. Even though this strategy had cost him his marriage, he couldn't think of a single thing he'd rather do. He grabbed the list of child homicides and headed for the door. Once in the car, he scanned the list for the three nearest addresses. Two were in the rough Detroit suburb of Taylor Michigan, unrelated and nine years apart, and one was near Ann Arbor, the oldest and most high profile case in the last two decades. He was a street cop when he first heard the story of young Aaron Reynolds being brutally murdered in the farm country near Ann Arbor. The case was never solved, and the father, after years of mourning, had picked up the pieces and done quite well for himself financially. Jamie decided to bypass Taylor and head to the Reynolds farm . . . A chance to meet one of the richest men in the United States was too tantalizing. Maybe he could get some free advice on where to invest his 401-K. As he drove, he pondered the situation with Kate . . . *Was she really at a baby shower and where was the agent Martinez?* He turned on to Interstate 96 and brought the black unmarked charger up to cruising speed. The big Hemi growled under the hood, and Jamie showed his appreciation by offering it more fuel . . . In no time, the orange neon Speedo was registering triple digits.

The more he thought about Super Hair touching Kate, the faster he went.

In no time, he reached the Interstate 23 turn off and headed south to mid-Michigan farm country and the Reynolds farm. The smell of fresh cut hay making its way through the charger's vent system prompted Jamie to roll down the windows and turn off the air. He turned on to a gravel road that had clearly been abandoned by the state of Michigan's highway department. Displaced gravel and two bare tracks in the middle of the road hinted of regular use, but Jamie had a hard time imagining this horse trail leading him to the home of the famous financial wizard, Aaron Reynolds. Wild raspberry bushes and mustard weed seemed to be fighting for dominance on the ditch bank, both encroaching into the roadside but reluctant or unable to breach the hard gravel path.

Suddenly, the road ended at a hard, red clay parking area in front of a modest, well-maintained two-story farmhouse. A well-fed black lab waddled out to greet Jamie, followed casually by two much leaner feline companions. Jamie glanced at his watch; 1:30 p.m. on a midsummer day was not a great time to catch a rich bachelor at home, but he hoped for the best as he exited the charger to meet the informal welcoming committee. He let the big dog carefully smell his outstretched hand as the two mousers did figure eights between his legs. After carefully inspecting his hand, the old dog lowered his head, giving Jamie the green light to scratch his ears. After allowing his head to be scratched for the prescribed amount of time, the big canine turned on his heels and waddled toward the front door. He stopped momentarily and gave a woof-snort to the two young cats, apparently informing them that their services were no longer needed.

The two cats broke ranks and bounded off towards the high grass like a couple of privates who had just received a day pass from their commander. The dog looked thoughtfully at Jamie for a moment, wagged its tail, and resumed its march towards the house. At the front door, the old lab dropped on the grass in the shadow of an old lilac bush. Jamie walked up the steps and glanced back at the old dog, who was watching him intently. His big tail beat the ground three times, then three more. Jamie finally got the hint and knocked on the door three times. As he waited for someone to answer the door, he looked around the property. An old non-functioning windmill stood overlooking the estate, while a fifty-something Chevy truck sat rusting quietly beside a chicken coop. Three older out buildings and the chicken coop accompanied the farmhouse in what would truly have been a Norman Rockwell painting, had it not been for the brand new pole barn constructed directly behind the old house. *It just seemed unnecessary, out of place,* Jamie thought to himself, *plenty of storage space in the three other buildings.*

Jamie walked around to the back of the house and surveyed the yard. He tried the door on the pole barn; it was locked. He turned around to find the old lab eyeing him suspiciously. "Easy there, big boy," Jamie said as he retreated back to the front of the house. As he made his way down the walk path that led to the charger, something caught his eye . . . Parked in the back of one of the larger buildings was an old rusty van . . . Still visible on the side were the letters "R&D Construction."

He considered walking over to investigate but decided against pushing his luck with the old dog further. He got in the charger and started down the stone road, pondering the unsightly pole barn and wondering why the rusty van seemed oddly familiar.

One by one, various business people and local Michigan celebrities made their way to the podium to hand deliver their donations . . . as their friends, family, and business associates remained at their host tables, sipping wine and taking photos of the presentations. Soon it would be Libby's turn to address the crowd on behalf of Reynolds & Reynolds. As they waited . . . Aaron made small talk with Raymond about his job and the Tigers' chances of another

World Series bid. Soon baseball conversation turned to Little Ray.

"So what do you think Little Ray's chances of making the traveling team are?" Aaron asked.

Just then, Susan's sister called Libby to the podium to address the crowd on behalf of Reynolds & Reynolds and present their donation.

As Aaron and Raymond turned their attention to the front, Raymond whispered back over his shoulder to his father-in-law, "Where you been? Little Ray's already on the team. He was one of the first picks."

Time seemed to freeze as Aaron processed the information . . . He watched Libby walking toward the stage as people began to applaud and give a standing ovation. Aaron grabbed his son-in-law with a steely grip as they too stood . . . "Libby told me he was going to try-outs today!" he hissed, attracting the attention of more than a few people in their immediate vicinity.

Raymond, startled by his father-in-law's reaction, said, "Wow, Dad! Relax. I have no idea why she would say that. Try-outs were a month ago!" By then, most of the people in the front, including Libby, knew something was amiss. The rest of the crowd slowly seated themselves.

As Aaron still stood, he whispered in Raymond's ear, "If he's not at try-outs, Raymond, *where is he*"

Raymond glanced at Libby, then at Aaron . . . "When we left the house, he was getting his gear around to go fishing," he said. "That's what he always does on Saturday."

Aaron looked at Libby, then around the room . . . Every eye was on him. In slow motion, he tried to untangle himself from the table and chairs. Drinks spilled and people cursed as he struggled to extricate himself from the crowd . . . . What moments ago was a wonderful nucleus of well wishers had become a tangle of obstacles . . . Even after he made his way to the foyer, he felt like he was moving in slow motion . . . "Get to the car . . . get to the river," he mumbled over and over to himself like a mantra . . . hoping the spoken word would hasten his progress.

Sparks flew from the undercarriage of the luxury sedan as it exited the parking garage like an overweight bucking bull leaves the shoot at a rodeo, trying desperately to get momentum without much visible success. Aaron avoided the main street as he crossed town, hoping to bypass the usual Saturday morning traffic . . . More than once, he narrowly avoided a serious collision as he blew through intersection after intersection. In less than fifteen minutes, he reached the entrance to the park, barely slowing to make the turn. The big Mercury rocked and swayed as he negotiated the intersection and powered down the winding park road that led to the boat docks. He thought about Aaron Jr. and the terror he felt when everyone finally realized his son was truly missing. The same terror he now felt magnified by ten . . . because of his intimate knowledge of its potential . . . like an old terrible friend who just shows up on your doorstep unannounced.

He screeched across the parking lot to the far end and glanced to the boat docks . . . empty except for a scattering of bicycles. He leapt from the car and ran down to the slip where he kept the boat for the summer . . . nothing! His head was spinning as he looked at the haphazard arrangement of bikes, apparently hastily abandoned . . . *Think, damn it!* He ran to the water's edge . . . then down the bank toward the willow grove . . . nothing! *Think!* He ran back towards the river, catching his foot on an old protruding root in the process. He fell headlong to the ground . . . hard enough to rattle his teeth . . . He shook his head and looked out across the dark river to the far bank . . . Slowly his head began to clear . . . A feeling of dread began to envelop his heart . . . The river road . . . he had seen the maroon Cadillac disappear down the dead-end logging trail only three weeks ago. He had chosen not to follow. Instead, he had driven home, pondering the meaning of the man's foray down the dirty road in his shiny car . . . He pulled himself to his feet and ran towards the car as the answer came to him. The man in the Cadillac had been looking for a secluded place to commit an unthinkable act! Invisible shackles weighed Aaron down as he ran towards the car . . . He was sure it would fail to start or the tires would be flat, either one of which would tip the scale of life and death, he was certain . . . He did not believe in death clocks or inevitable destiny . . . The future was constantly changing, evolving, becoming the present. The car was where he had left it, the tires were full, and the engine roared to life.

Aaron reached the old river road without incident . . . which was a miracle considering it was a Saturday morning in late July. Normally, the park was packed with people picnicking and canoeing . . . but that day, the park was not busy . . . like it had been closed to the public so this drama could unfold. Dust rose behind him like a great storm as he bounced down the river road . . . As he entered the dark canopy that skirted the river's edge, the storm, stifled by the thick foliage, did not follow, and the stone road gave way to packed red sand and pine needles. He slowed the car as his eyes adjusted to this new dark world . . . He followed the road for about a mile, almost getting stuck twice in the deepest ruts . . . Soon a vehicle came into view. But to his dismay, it was not a maroon Cadillac but a shiny new SUV. He parked beside it and quickly got out . . . a trail head was marked by an old cedar post with an aluminum DNR tag wrapped around the top. He glanced around the immediate area and found nothing suspicious. Slowly, he circled the SUV . . . Dark tinted windows gave no hint to the contents in the low-light conditions. As he reached the back, he saw the license plate, California JLY 5674, Evan McGregor's plate. He broke for the trail head on a run, churning up sand and pine needles as he went . . . He ran hard for a couple of hundred yards and was just about to scream Raymond's name when he broke into a small clearing . . . All three boys sat facing the river . . . their poles rested in makeshift forks pruned from nearby trees. Behind them, sitting casually on the ground . . . was Evan McGregor. Beside him was a black nylon duffel bag.

Ray was the first to speak, "Hey, Grandpa, how'd you find us? We're cat-fishing! This is Mick's favorite spot!"

Aaron turned as Evan stood and extended his hand. "Hi," he said with a casual smile, "I'm Mick . . . Mick Evans . . . I was just showing the boys an old fishing hole of mine. Hope you don't mind."

Aaron quickly assessed the situation . . . The boys were safe . . . He was unarmed. The Mercury he had driven to the banquet didn't even have a weapon in it. If he did not play this right, if he showed any suspicion at all, Evan McGregor could pull a gun and kill them all as they made their way back to the car. He shook Evan's hand like an old friend.

"I'm Ray's grandpa . . . just an old worry wart, I guess . . . Hey, did you blindfold these boys before you took 'em to your favorite fishing hole? That's what you're supposed to do," he said, laughing heartily . . . "Come on, boys. I'll give you a ride back to your bikes. Gonna be dark in a couple hours." As the boys readied their equipment for the hike out, Aaron chanced a glance at Evan. He was looking down at his duffel bag . . . like he was contemplating his next move . . . A look of disappointment mixed with indecision etched his face. As the boys filed out of the clearing, Aaron motioned for Evan to go ahead of him. "I'll take up the rear," he said . . . Evan seemed to consider this. He looked at Aaron squarely in the face, looking for any hint of suspicion or deception . . . Aaron met his gaze with clear eyes . . . and an easy smile . . . Without a word, Evan turned and made his way down the trail . . .

CHAPTER 15

Time to Act

L IBBY'S FIRST WAKING thought was of her father. She stared up at the ceiling fan. Oak paddles with brass trim slowly stirred the smells of a Midwest morning. The aroma of cinnamon rolls apparently cooling on the kitchen counter drifted through the bedroom door as damp, musky man scent oozed from the master bath . . . They mingled together above her, along with the scent of morning breath, not so fresh sheets, and lilacs from the open window . . . The combined aroma oddly enough reminded her of Mr. Meeks, the baker, who often doused himself with cheap cologne mid-morning to cover the smells of a man who had been working hard for many hours before his first sleepy-eyed customer stumbled in to purchase his sweet delights. The endless circular stroke of oaken oars, along with the sweet-sour smell of Mr. Meeks, caused her head to spin. She closed her eyes again . . . remembering the scene her father had caused the day before. The flood of inquiries that had followed his hasty departure, some honest and sincere, others probing for scandal, had almost overwhelmed her. Thank goodness for Susan and her sister, who managed somehow to wrap up the formalities of the fund-raiser and give Raymond and her a ride home, where they waited for Ray Jr to return. When he finally arrived, driven by his grandfather, she went out to meet them. Little Ray barely acknowledged her as he bounced past, headed for the house with a stringer of fish to show his dad.

As Aaron retrieved Ray's bike from the trunk, he started to say something to Libby, but she halted him in mid-sentence with a curt wave of her hand. They stared at each other for long time, trying to convey thoughts without speaking, a raised brow . . . a half-frown . . . a nervous purging of air through flared nostrils . . . (How could you . . . I'm sorry . . . You embarrassed me . . . I know I did . . .)

Without saying a word, she took the bike from her father and pushed it towards the garage. Only when she heard the car start up again did she glance back . . . Her father was looking at himself in the rearview mirror . . . *What did he see?* she wondered . . . *A man standing at a precipice, about to fall into despair again . . . Where had her confident, reborn father gone? . . . And who was this paranoid stranger in the mirror?* Without taking his eyes off the mirror, Aaron put the car in reverse and backed slowly out of the driveway. He paused for a second in the middle of the road, as if considering whether to wave or not wave. Libby half-raised her hand . . . in case her father chose to wave. He did not. Instead . . . he stole a glance at the man in the mirror . . . and drove away.

The man kneeling by the campfire was vaguely familiar. He looked different than Aaron remembered. Sure, thirty pounds was missing from his frame and he was twenty years younger . . . but his face seemed brighter, clearer, like a new penny. The Au Sable River flowing behind him also looked different . . . cleaner, unmolested by the foul run-off of the many small companies that by necessity started popping up across Michigan in the mid-seventies to supply ball joints, seat frames, and air-conditioning lines to feed the great Detroit automotive giants. Any part that could be farmed out allowed more resources to be focused solely on engine blocks and chassis. The river no longer flowed crystal clear but a murky green, anti-freeze color, sometimes leaning towards a rusty green when the massive foundries were forging more iron than aluminum. The woman in the photo was a rare, petite beauty. The country song "She Don't Know She's Beautiful" came to mind, as it always did when he held the old dog-eared photo in his hands. She had on khaki shorts and her dark ponytail was pulled through the back of an old tan ball cap. She stood straight, hands on her hips, watching Aaron cook trout with a satisfied smile as two small children sat on their haunches, arms crossed, also watching intently, waiting.

Aaron held the family photo to his chest and closed his eyes, trying to remember his wife's rare beautiful smile . . . The first time he saw it, he had been trapped like a raccoon in the porch light; he could not look away. Slowly and carefully, she had drawn him into her embrace, whispering words of encouragement along the way. It had been the last dance of the night. Even when the band had stopped playing, they had continued to move across the floor, laughing and whispering in each other's ear, swaying to a beat that only they could hear. He had not been looking for love, but love had found him. Together they had built a life, raised two beautiful children, and started a small construction business. Each hurdle they faced as one drew them closer together. He tried to remember what it felt like to hold her in his arms and feel the cares of life fall impotent at their feet, small and insignificant in the shadow of their combined love.

Aaron carefully slid the old photo back into the manila envelope from which it came and put the half-torn flap carefully back in place. He folded the one remaining aluminum ear over to secure the flap and placed the envelope back in the box.

Next, he picked up a framed picture of Aaron Jr holding an impossibly large Louisville slugger, the one he always insisted on bringing to practice on team photo day. His hair was sandy, with streaks of blond highlights that only appeared in late July. They blossomed for a month or two, then faded away with the Michigan summer.

How old would he be now? Aaron thought. Estimating his age in the photo at eight and adding sixteen years, Aaron tried to imagine the boy in the photo standing in front of him, a tall, strong, twenty-four-year-old. He couldn't conjure up the image. It reminded him of the time when he was a boy and started to see advertisements on television for a new cartoon called Spiderman. All they showed was a big fierce spider casting a web, while the catchphrase played over and over (Spiderman, Spider man, does whatever a spider can . . .). The brilliant marketing ploy by Marvel Comics whipped young boys into a frenzy, climbing over bus seats and school desks, while young girls drew pictures of their latest beaus, adding six or eight legs protruding from various parts of their bodies. Everyone was trying to imagine what

Spiderman must look like. When the comic finally aired, it was almost a letdown . . . skinny guy in a red and blue suit. Aaron looked at the photo again, twenty-four years old, the image would not come. Even if it had, he was sure it would also be a letdown. Aaron Reynolds Jr would always be nine years old. He would not age. He could not age. He hadn't been allowed to age. Moisture formed in the corner of Aaron's eye. His forehead creased with pain. Tension growing inside him caused his shoulders to shudder, and a single tear was born. It rolled down his cheek and lost momentum in the unfamiliar day-old growth on his chin. It slowly ambled right, then left, then focused on an old slight scar, where no facial hair would grow. It followed the scar to the cleft of his chin and paused for only a moment, gathering its meager resources before the final leap to where tears go. An ocean of pain, a river of anguish. Without fanfare, it leaped into space, landing on the framed photo of his son with an audible plop! It ran diagonally an inch across the photo from left to right and ended where the bat rested on his son's shoulder. Aaron tilted the picture in the light. The thick, salty, translucent solution seemed to cause a distortion of the photo . . . making his son's face look off-center or disconnected, causing Aaron to remember how he died, the final horrific image of his beloved son.

A fire slowly began to rekindle inside him . . . a fire he had learned could dry up tears . . . a fire that had forged a new life for him. It had tempered him and made him strong. He let the fire build slowly until he was sure of its commitment to consume. It was time to act . . . time to stand at the gate and welcome another. Evan McGregor was a pedophile, a child killer. Aaron was sure he was responsible for the murder of the boy in Saline and probably many more. He had seen the rape kit in his trunk. If Aaron allowed him to leave the city, children would die. He put the box of pictures away, slipped outside, and made his way to the chamber. He had preparations to make.

The wheels of justice were known to turn slow, but this is ridiculous, Kate thought as she waited outside the judge's chambers. A child killer was roaming the state, and she was sitting in the foyer waiting on paperwork, crossing t's and dotting i's. As she waited, she thought about Jamie. She knew he was feeling put off by the young FBI agent, which was ridiculous really. If she fell for every young agent that winked at her, she would never accomplish anything. The thing that attracted her to Jamie was not necessarily his looks, though he was not at all hard on the eyes. It was his calm confidence, his ability to act and react under extreme pressure. That was what Kate found sexy about Jamie. Truth of the matter was that most of the agents she knew would probably shoot themselves in the foot if a real shoot-out were to occur. What really was becoming a wedge between them was this Gatekeeper thing. Ever since his abduction, Jamie had become obsessed with catching him. It was like he was ashamed that this unknown vigilante had been able to outsmart the great Detective James Larson. His cop ego had been deeply scarred. Joe Public was not supposed to interfere with the pursuit of justice . . . and the Gatekeeper was doing just that. He was dispatching pedophiles like it was his job and had taken Jamie out of circulation for forty-eight hours like someone would put a misbehaving pup in a kennel for some quiet time.

She couldn't even talk to Jamie about the Saline homicide. It was like it was irrelevant to him. She could still see that young boy's sneaker hanging in the brush and often had nightmares filled with visions of the young boy's death mask, no longer silenced by the limitations of this world. In her dream world, he had a voice. He could scream and plead, to his killer for mercy, to her for justice, and always to the Gatekeeper for vengeance . . . An entity known to him only in her dream world, she was sure. Often, she would wake covered in sweat, feeling hopeless, unable to help him, hindered by the shackles of the law, by the morality of the masses, and by the oaths she had taken. Without fail, as she lay in the dark waiting for her heartbeat to steady, she thought of the Gatekeeper. He did not wait for paperwork, he was not paralyzed by the anesthesia of tree-hugging liberals. Many times, she prayed for his continued success and for his ability to evade capture. She feared for him; he was being pursued by a formidable foe in Detective James Larson. Even then, Jamie was downtown, trying to make a connection with Aaron Reynolds, working the grieving parent angle to the last possible lead.

Finally, a clerk emerged with the Evan McGregor warrant in hand. The clerk informed her it was strictly limited to financial records. Anything more would require additional warrants. Kate thanked the clerk and made her way to the car, warrant in hand, feeling oddly empowered by the flimsy document. She hoped to spend the rest of the afternoon trying to get a location on Evan McGregor or the vehicle described by the Gatekeeper during his anonymous call. Maybe it was the female in her, the still dormant, maternal material in her DNA, not yet formed by the pressure of childbirth, that made her more interested in catching a child murderer than a pedophile killer. Perhaps her heart believed the nightmares would stop if the child killer was caught . . . or killed . . . She did not know. What she did know was that the Gatekeeper was her ally. In some kindred spirit alternate reality, they had similar goals, to silence the young boy in her dreams and make sure real screams no longer echoed through the dark Michigan woods. The Gatekeeper had not injured her cop ego, and she was unwilling to allow Jamie's offense to become her own . . . even if they were partners.

CHAPTER 16

The Patriot

THE REYNOLDS & Reynolds firm was buzzing with activity Monday afternoon when Jamie walked in. People moved from cubicle to cubicle comparing graphs and talking in hushed tones as five hundred-dollar suits entered and exited the elevators, their hosts wearing either penny loafers or high heels. *The ratio appeared to be about one to one,* Jamie thought to himself, a very balanced work force compared to the Special Crimes Unit, which had about two women to every ten men. Jamie made his way to the reception area and introduced himself to the most beautiful redhead he had ever seen. "Hi, my name is

Detective James Larson . . . I'm here to see Libby Reynolds. I believe she is expecting me."

After a brief phone conversation, the receptionist put down the receiver and said, "Mrs Reynolds is expecting you . . . Suit 1, fourth floor."

Jamie thanked her as he stole his second handful of cinnamon mints. As the etched glass and stainless steel elevator doors closed, Jamie envisioned the old farmhouse . . . home of Aaron Reynolds. *No trappings of wealth there,* he thought as he studied the hand-polished cherry interior of the elevator. He was sure he would like Aaron Reynolds if he ever had the chance to meet him. His phone number was a closely guarded secret and part of the reason for that day's meeting with his only surviving child. The fourth chime sounded as the doors opened to a short hallway that led to two, large, cherry doors. Longer hallways led to the left and the right. Single cherry doors lined each hallway. Each door had a suite number and a name emblazoned on brass plates. The slightly, but noticeably, larger brass plate above the cherry doors in front of him read: "Mrs Libby Lombardo Reynolds." He pushed down on the brass handle and entered yet another reception area. A round-faced woman apparently named Mary, if you believed the many framed documents that filled the wall behind her, gave Jamie a cheery welcome and quickly informed Mrs. Reynolds via wireless intercom that her 1:30 was on time. Jamie took a seat in a comfortable chair while he waited to see Mrs. Libby Lombardo Reynolds. A framed copy of *Forbes* magazine sat on an end table near the chair. Jamie picked it up and examined it. The man on the cover had piercing blue eyes and a calm confident smile . . . a sharp contrast to the old newspaper clippings showing a grief-stricken father addressing reporters while consoling his wife.

Libby Reynolds came around the corner, her hand extended. She greeted Jamie with a warm smile. "That's my father," she said warmly, "taken last year after our company make the top one hundred."

"I see," Jamie said, wondering what that meant exactly.

"Follow me, Mr. Larson. Would you like a drink? Coke? Water?"

"No, I'm fine," Jamie said as she led him into a spacious office modestly decorated in earth tone colors, with lots of copper ornamentation on the walls and desk furnishings.

After Jamie was seated, Libby sat down, clasped her hands together on her desk, and asked, "How can I help you, Mr. Larson?"

"Well Mrs. Reynolds, I am investigating the death of your brother almost fifteen years ago now . . . I'm sure it was a very hard time for you, and I regret having to bring it up after all this time, but I was wondering if I could go over a few things with you?"

Libby looked a little let down but quickly recovered. "I'm sorry, Mr. Larson. I was sure you were here for something financially related and was excited at the prospect of defending this institution's integrity. We are very proud of our company and keep very rigid, ethical checks and balances in place."

"I'm sorry," Jamie replied. "When I requested this meeting, I didn't mention my Special Crimes Unit credentials. I guess I thought I'd have a better chance of seeing you if your curiosity was piqued"

"Well," Libby said, "it was unnecessary but it worked. Matter of fact, my curiosity is still piqued. My brother has been gone for fifteen years. The last time I talked to an officer about him was ten years ago, when a cold case detective called with a few inquiries. Unfortunately, nothing ever came of his investigation, and nothing more was heard. The general consensus is the killer is probably in prison or dead. Would you concur with that scenario, Mr. Larson? And please call me Libby."

"Well, Libby, the records show that many pedophiles die of old age . . . but violent pedophilic killers . . . tend to get caught or killed in five years or less. This is due to the escalation in their crimes. It's like they are trying to catch up on a lifetime of fantasizing in as short a time as possible. This often leads to their capture or demise by some other means related to their deviant lifestyle. So in answer to your question, I would say, yes, your brother's killer is probably long dead, most likely killed in prison by another inmate, who he made the mistake of sharing his sexual preferences with. It happens all the time."

"I see," Libby said. "I suppose I should take peace in knowing that, but I'd still like to look at his face . . . to see what a monster looks like. He caused my family so much pain. I'd like to address him in court on behalf of my mother and family and make him hear how much damage he has caused, then listen to my father tell him what a wonderful son Aaron was and how much we all loved him. It's really a good thing they never caught him, I guess. A year after Aaron was killed, when I was home from college, my father and I were talking, and he confided in me that if Aaron's killer was ever caught and proven guilty, that he might consider taking justice into his own hands. I asked him what he meant . . . He just shrugged it off and gave me the father-daughter, stop-drop-and-scream speech. That's what he always told me to do if anyone ever tried to abduct me."

Jamie sat forward in his seat. "So your father was suggesting he might take matters into his own hands if the opportunity ever arose?"

"Yes, I guess you could say that," Libby replied soberly, feeling like she had just let an unknown cat out of an unseen bag and wishing she could somehow put it back.

Jamie paused as he considered his next question . . . "Libby, do you think that your father is capable of violence, if this situation or one similar to it were to arise?"

Libby looked at Jamie. She sat back in her chair and crossed her legs. "You're not here to talk to me about my brother, are you, Detective?"

Cadillac Man

The suite at the top of the Marriott building looked like a college fraternity hazing had taken place. Liquor and wine bottles lay about the floor, and two cigars lay melted into the tinted Plexiglas top of the coffee table. A briefcase lay open, its contents spread across the table and about the room. In the center of the collage of Polaroid photos, propped up sideways against a complimentary miniature liquor bottle, was a photo of three boys standing together smiling. Each clutched a fishing pole tightly in his hand, the green river flowed behind them. Evan lay on the couch staring at it. Dark rings circled tired eyes, a gray bristled shadow covered half his face. It was to have been his "before" photo, to be followed by an "after" photo. There was always an "after" photo. A deep moan emanated from inside him. Slowly, it started to sound more like a growl, a throaty warning of bad things to come. He should have gutted the intruder like a fish and had his way with the boys and had actually considered doing just that. What had stopped him? Not fear. The man was no bigger than he and was clearly unarmed. What had he seen in his face? Nothing that gave warning of suspicion. If he had seen that, they would all be dead, and Evan would be miles away, reliving the excitement of the encounter and planning his next. *Recognition!* That was what had stopped him. The piercing blue eyes, the scar on the cleft of his chin, he had seen the man before, and that realization had paralyzed him, hindering his ability to act. All the way to the car, he tried to make the connection. Slowly, the alcoholic fog in his head was burned off by the conscious thought of a new day. *The drunk! The stumbler! The poor actor! The man he had found leaning against his car behind the Marriot . . . the one he thought he saw closing his trunk . . . Was this his unseen meddler . . . his tormentor? The one who had purchased a remote for his car? How had this man possibly found him a mile and a half down the old river road on an unused foot path? Unless!* Evan didn't realize he was still growling until his throat involuntarily constricted and issued a final dry squeak! *The Gatekeeper!*

He sat upright and hastily started picking up the photos and putting them in the briefcase . . . *the Gatekeeper! It had to be him . . . it all made sense now.* Evan picked up the phone and called the main desk. "This is Evan McGregor, Room 1501. I regret to inform you that I'll be leaving this evening. I have some banking to attend to, then I'll be back to gather my things. Looks like I'm going to have a coffee table to pay for, had a bit of a party last night. While I'm gone, have someone assess the damage. Deduct it from the cash advance I made. I'll pick up the balance when I check out." Evan did not wait for a reply but made his way to the shower. He needed to clear his head and gather his thoughts. He needed to be gone. He had lingered there too long.

Libby waited quietly for Jamie's response.

"Well," he said, "yes . . . I am here to talk to you about your brother's murder. Specifically, I'm looking into unsolved child homicides that have occurred over the last fifteen years. Your brother's is one of the last on my list. I'm trying to eliminate possible suspects."

"I don't understand," Libby said.

Jamie sat up in his chair and scratched the back of his head absently as he stretched. "Well, I might as well just say it. You've been very helpful, Libby, and I will not take much more of your time. I am investigating the Gatekeeper slayings. We believe the Gatekeeper could be a grieving parent. Are you familiar with the case?"

"Yes," Libby said guardedly, "I have loosely followed the details in the local media."

"Well," Jamie said, "I'd like to talk to your father in person but have been unable to contact him as yet. So I'll ask you point blank . . . Do you think your father is capable of rendering this kind of vigilante justice? Is there anything about his recent activities that would arouse your suspicions in this regard?"

Libby got up and walked over to a wet bar. She poured herself half a glass of bourbon and took a long drink. As she did, she considered Jamie's question. Her mind replayed the events of the last few days . . . her father's hasty departure from the banquet, his obsession with Ray Jr, and the odd way he had stared at himself in the mirror only yesterday. Suddenly, her heart ached for him. He had been through so much, and against all odds, he had succeeded and prospered. She turned back to Jamie and addressed him formally, "Detective Larson, my father is one of the most capable men you will ever meet. There is nothing he cannot accomplish. He has risen from the depths of despair to build this company and rebuild our family. There is nothing he cannot do. Is he a killer? No, I don't believe he is. Would he avenge my brother's death given the opportunity? I cannot say. I will have to let him answer that question himself. I will give him your number, Detective Larson, and have him call you in the next couple of days. Will that work?"

Jamie stood and extended his hand. "That will be fine, Mrs. Reynolds, and thank you so much for your time . . . Oh, and if you think of anything else, anything at all, please call me any time." He reached into his coat pocket and produced a card. Libby took it, stepped back to her desk, and retrieved one of her own. She gave it to Jamie. "Likewise," she said.

Jamie turned and walked to the door while reading the card. Embossed on the front it said "Reynolds & Reynolds Financial, Eleanor Reynolds, Vice President." Jamie paused at the door with his hand on the handle, looking at the card. Libby waited for the question she knew was coming. "Eleanor Reynolds," Jamie said. "How do you get Libby from Eleanor? Wouldn't it be more like Ellie Reynolds?"

Libby laughed. The question seemed to clear the air. "Well, Detective Larson, my father is quite the patriot, always has been. I was born during the Iranian Hostage Situation. My father said he watched on the hospital television screen as the American hostages were released. He was so excited that he picked me up and said, 'Liberty! Eleanor Liberty Reynolds! That's what we'll call you.' I hated it in school, always having to recount the story I just told you. But I like it now, makes me feel proud, patriotic. Maybe that's what my father intended."

Jamie looked at her smiling face. "I like it too," he said. "Thanks again, Libby. Please have your father call me at his convenience." As he closed the door, he couldn't help feeling more admiration for the man he had yet to meet in person.

CHAPTER 17

The Chamber

ONE BY ONE, the detectives left for the evening. A few stayed over finishing their reports. All things considered, it had been an uneventful Monday. Jamie and Kate had ordered a pizza and were planning to pull a night shift. Captain Wells was planning another press conference on the Gatekeeper slayings Wednesday, and they had nothing to offer. Agent Martinez had departed to wherever it was that FBI agents went when cases cooled off, and Jamie was looking forward to spending a quiet evening with Kate, even if it was at work. The goal that evening was to review the information they already had, piece by piece, eliminating anything not essential to the case. They both sat in Jamie's office. On the walls were photos of the Gatekeeper's victims and the Saline homicide, along with two lists of known methods of operation or MOs. On one list was information known to the public. On the other list was information that had not yet been released to the public. It was a short one, as reporters were constantly sleuthing around, connecting the dots doing their own investigative work. Like a week after the last Gatekeeper victim was found, the *Ann Arbor Times* reporter Michael Donovan reported that it appeared that the victims of the Gatekeeper were being dumped in the same locations where they had disposed of the bodies of their young victims. Had that information been withheld from the public, they might have been able to catch the Gatekeeper dumping a body if the perp's disappearance was reported soon enough. The only thing left on the non-public list was the fact that each victim had the Roman numeral "IV" and the word "justice" carved into the left pectoral muscle over the heart. Also on that list was the information Jamie had gleaned while he was abducted; middle-aged male, Caucasian, highly intelligent.

The desk below the photos was covered with dozens of different files . . . all related to the case. The homicide in Saline was on top, along with two dozen child homicides that had occurred in the area over the last fifteen years. Included with these was the Aaron Reynolds Jr case. Jamie had added a few pages to it that afternoon after talking to

Libby. While he had been downtown, Kate had looked into the Evan McGregor financial records . . . to no avail. It appeared that Evan McGregor chose to use prepaid debit cards that were less traceable and even more frequently used cash whenever possible to purchase cars, gas, and necessaries. Kate believed that if they could find Evan McGregor, the Gatekeeper would be nearby. Jamie wasn't so sure, but he feigned interest when she came across a bit of information on McGregor, which she just had. Apparently, they were no longer looking for a maroon Cadillac coupe. After running the plate, she found out that the same plate was now registered to a black Escalade. The registration gave no indication as to where the vehicle was at present, because it was still registered in California. So the only way to find out where the Escalade was at that time was to physically put eyes on it.

Jamie looked at the photos. "Four justice," he said to himself, ". . . for justice! Yes, it was justice all right. Each perp died in the same way he had committed his crimes. What's with the Roman numeral IV, though? Is he trying to tell us there will ultimately be four victims?" Jamie thought not. He suspected the man would continue to kill until he ran out of bad guys or got caught. Jamie handed the Aaron Reynolds Jr file to Kate and picked up the Saline homicide file. "Better get started," he said. "It's going to be a long night."

They both got comfortable and started to leaf through their individual files, looking for key words or phrases, trying to see, without looking, to perceive, without understanding. The answer lay in front of them, Jamie was sure. It was like looking for a needle in a haystack. If you looked too hard, you'd never see it. If you dive in the haystack, it just might poke you in the ass.

Cadillac Man

After transferring the funds he had made from the sale of his father's stocks to a trusted family bank in Berkeley, Evan had gone back to his room and waited for night to fall. He liked traveling at night. The harsh light of day exposed too much. It left no room for imagination. Glance into a dark alley at night, and the possibilities were endless. Look into the same alley during the light of day and see garbage and decay. Yes, darkness knocked the rough edges off everything: women, real estate, one's own reflection in a dark storefront window . . . but mostly, it made colors deeper, richer. Black was only truly black at night. And blood . . . blood was not even worth looking at during the day, almost fluorescent in color, making his work look like broken dolls painted haphazardly with cheap red barn paint. But at night, blood flowed dark and crimson, warm and reflective. Outside the motel window, the light had retreated to the west, leaving the city to fend for itself with halogen and neon, both of which created more shadows than light, painting a world of dark images on a dimly lit orange and green cityscape.

Evan picked up his briefcase, then pulled out the handle on his small carry-on. He took one last look around the room. The coffee table had been replaced and the room had been cleaned meticulously. The next day, he would be a thousand miles away. He stepped into the elevator and made his way to the lobby. When he reached the back door, he stood looking out at the night for a long time, looking for anything out of place, any sign of movement. He pushed the automatic opener and stepped out under the security light. Again, he waited, watching, listening. He hit the unlock button, walked quickly to the back of the Cadillac, and lifted the hatch. As he stepped forward to put his suitcase in the back, he felt a sickening squish beneath his right foot. He reached down and touched the bottom of his shoe. He brought his hand back up to his nose and grunted with disgust, dog shit! "Are you kidding me?" he said out loud. He stepped over into the grass beside the parking lot and did a bad imitation of a Michael Jackson moonwalk, trying to rid both shoes of the canine crud. He smelt his hand. "Unbelievable," he growled. He walked to the passenger side, opened the door, and leaned in to get a Kleenex out of the glove box. As he did, he realized he had let his guard down completely! Before he could react, he heard a slight scuffing sound on the pavement behind him, and everything went black . . .

Aaron handcuffed the unconscious man and sat him in the passenger seat. He went to the rear, avoiding the greasy canine feces he had strategically placed there. He put the two bags in the rear and jumped in the driver's seat. Slowly, he pulled into the dark alley, followed it to the end of the block, and drove the back streets quietly out of town towards the farm.

Evan McGregor woke with a start to total darkness. *Where am . . . Where was I? . . . What day is this?* . . . As he pondered those questions, he realized he was not alone. Someone was sitting in the darkness. He could hear the steady breathing. The room felt cool for a July night. Evan did not yet trust his voice to speak with authority, so he felt around with his hands quietly. He was secured to a chair of some kind, with leather straps at his chest and elbows, allowing only a minimal amount of room to move and breathe, which he did slowly and steadily until he felt able to speak. "OK," he said, "what now? I'm sure there has been some kind of mistake. If it's money you're after, I am a very wealthy man." He let the echoes of his last words fade before saying more. "You'll find over $50,000 in my vehicle. It's hidden in the side panels. Your welcome to it. All I'll do is shake your hand and drive away." Evan waited for a response, confident that his generous offer was too good to turn down.

It was close to midnight when Jamie and Kate decided to call it a night. They had trimmed the number of useful files down to about twenty. Still, they had no suspects, no leads, and no information to feed Captain Wells for his news conference. Jamie stepped back and looked at the wall. Kate watched him intently.

"Four justice," he said out loud, "justice!" Jamie reached in his pocket and took out the card Libby Reynolds had given him earlier that day. He took out his cell phone and dialed the home number on the gold embossed card.

"Hello," a male voice said sleepily.

"Sorry to bother you. This is Detective James Larson. I'd like to speak to Libby, if I may . . ."

A brief hushed conversation took place in the background before Jamie heard Libby's voice on the other end.

"Good morning, or good evening," she said. "Which is it, Detective Larson?"

"I am so sorry, Mrs. Reynolds. We've been working all night and something has come up. We'd like to clear it up before we call it a day"

"Can I go back to sleep if I answer correctly?" Libby asked.

"Absolutely!" Jamie said. "Libby, you said that your father said he might consider taking justice into his own hands if the man who killed your brother was ever caught. Did he use those exact words? I mean 'justice.' Is that a word he used often"

Libby could sense the urgency in Jamie's voice but had no idea what to make of it. "Well, Detective Larson, he did use the word "justice" probably two dozen times a day. Remember I told you my middle name is Liberty? Well, my brother's middle name was Justice. Aaron Justice Reynolds . . . like the pledge of allegiance, Liberty and Justice for all."

Jamie looked at the photos on the wall; the message carved deep into the flesh of each dead pedophile was not a ranting declaration but a humble explanation. Those men were killed because fifteen years ago, someone like them had killed an innocent nine-year-old boy named Aaron Justice Reynolds. They were killed for Justice! Jamie apologized to Libby for disturbing her at such a late hour and said good-bye. He closed his phone and looked at Kate.

"Let's go!"

"What? Where?" Kate said.

"To the Reynolds farm. His son's middle name was Justice. He's committing these crimes in the name of his murdered son! *For Justice!*" They both ran for the door.

"Should I call for back-up?" Kate asked.

"No," Jamie said, "he didn't harm me before. He has no beef with us. It's not us I'm worried about."

They got in the charger and headed for the Reynolds farm.

Cadillac Man

A bright light shone in Evan's face and a voice spoke. "I'm not interested in your money," the voice said. "Tell me about the boys at the river. What was your intent?"

Evan still did not yet have his wits about him and was frankly pissed off about his sore head and uncomfortable conditions. "That is none of your business!" he spat!

Aaron stepped into the light. "That is where you're mistaken!" he said. "One of those boys was my grandson. That makes it my business. How old are you?" Aaron asked.

"Fifty-two," Evan offered, intrigued by the new line of questioning.

"So you were born in 1960?" Aaron said as he walked back to the table.

"Yes, I believe that's the math," Evan said smugly.

Aaron picked up the briefcase and sat it on the edge of the table, where they could both see its contents when it was opened. He spun the four tumblers on the combination, then lined up the numbers 1, 9, 6, 0. He looked at Evan and hit the thumb clasp; it popped open with a satisfying click.

Aaron lifted the lid on the briefcase, revealing a thick stack of newspaper clippings. He lifted them on to the table and leafed through them. Each one told the same grim tale of abduction and murder, of ruined young lives. The sheer number was staggering. Near the top of the stack was an article about the boy from Saline. Aaron picked it up. "Tell me about Devin," he said.

"Who?" Evan said.

"The boy from Saline, the boy in the park. It says here he was stabbed multiple times and sexually assaulted."

The memory allowed Evan to transport himself away from his current unpleasant circumstances, if only for a moment. "Yes! I remember him," Evan said with a sly grin.

Aaron walked over to his work area. "It says here he was killed with a survival knife. Did it look like this?" Aaron asked, picking up a sheathed knife and walking back to the table. He slide the knife from the sheath and let Evan see the dark anodised finish and razor-sharp edge.

Evan refused to be intimidated. Instead, he played the money card again. "How much?"

Aaron ignored the question and turned back to the briefcase. One by one, he picked up the Polaroids. They were stapled together in sets of two. The front photo showed a young boy whose face was either smiling or full of question. The second photo without fail displayed human wreckage on a scale that Aaron had never seen before. One by one, he took each photo out, examined it, and laid it on the table.

"Five hundred thousand," Evan said.

Aaron continued his grim task. He was nearing the bottom of the stack and could tell the pictures were old by the coloration and sticky filmy residue on them. As he picked up one of the older pictures, his heart stopped. His breath caught in his lungs and he thought his legs might buckle. He held it up to the light. Looking up at him from the old yellow photo was the image of his son. His eyes looked confused, unsure, scared! He did not look at the second photo. He walked over and laid the photo on the work bench. He stared down at it.

"One million!" Evan McGregor snarled, unaware of the recent turn of events.

Jamie cut the lights as they pulled into the Reynolds farm. They both pulled their weapons as they exited the car. The house was dark and all was quiet except for the chorus of night sounds provided by the humid swamps that surrounded the property. In front of the unsightly pole barn sat a brand new black Escalade with California plates.

"I guess we found Evan McGregor," Jamie said to Kate.

They both exited the charger, quietly closing their doors. The door on the pole barn was slightly ajar. Jamie and Kate eased through the door. A full moon illuminated most of the garage. Jamie was reluctant to turn on the light and give their whereabouts away. So they waited inside the door until their eyes adjusted to the moonlit interior. Slowly, they worked their way to the back. Kate cursed as she bumped her head on a bicycle that was hanging from the ceiling. Jamie held his finger to his lips as they continued deeper into the pole barn. The silhouette of an old street rod came into view; it seem to be the only thing of interest in the mostly vacant building. Near the back, they stopped to consider their next course of action. Kate suggested that they clear the house one room at a time. Jamie started to say something, when they both heard a muffled voice yell.

"Two million, two million dollars!"

Jamie looked down for the source of the voice. An old piece of plywood, roughly two feet by two feet, lay on the floor. A loop of string in the middle served as a makeshift handle. It was counter-sunk into the floor, leaving Jamie to believe it was part of the original design of the pole barn, some kind of basement or crawl space.

CHAPTER 18

Final Justice

JAMIE CAREFULLY PICKED up the plywood door. A flood of light issued from the deep hole. He could see a ladder leading down.

Suddenly, a voice pleaded from the depths, "Help, please. Please help me . . ." Evan McGregor had seen the wooden cover lifted away, but the man in the corner was oblivious to what was happening. He had been in the corner for fifteen minutes, ignoring Evan's financial offers. Evan then focused his attention on whoever was standing above. "Hello! My name is Evan McGregor. I've been abducted. Please help me . . . now!"

Jamie yelled into the chamber, "Aaron Reynolds? . . . My name is Detective James Larson, Special Crimes Unit. I believe we've met before. Are you armed?"

Aaron seemed to snap out of his trance. "No, Detective Larson, I'm not armed. Come down."

"Aaron, I'm going to ask you to back up against the far wall and put your hands where I can see them. I'm coming down. My partner will be coming down after me. If anything happens to me, she calls SWAT and all bets are off! Do you understand?"

"I understand," Aaron said.

Jamie looked at Kate and shrugged. He stepped into the hole and made his way down the ladder. He reached the bottom and turned around. Aaron Reynolds leaned quietly against the far wall, nothing in his hands but a photo. A middle-aged man was strapped to a chair closer to Jamie. Immediately, he started demanding that Jamie release him and arrest Aaron. "He's nuts, I tell you! Crazy."

Kate made her way down the ladder and stood quietly behind Jamie, taking in the strange surroundings. It looked like a scene from *Silence of the Lambs.* Jamie held his revolver at his side as he made his way to the table and picked up a handful of newspaper clippings. After glancing at them, he passed them to Kate. He looked at Evan.

"Those aren't mine!" Evan said. "They're his!" he said, pointing at Aaron.

Jamie picked up a handful of Polaroids. He leafed through them, looking first at the front photo and then the back. He tried to be professional but could not help being shocked at what he saw. "Are these his also?" he asked Evan as he passed the photos to Kate.

Before Evan could speak, Aaron addressed Jamie, "There are thirty-six sets of photos in that briefcase. I took the briefcase out of his car, the code to the briefcase is birthdate, and I'm quite certain his DNA is on most of those photos, in one form or another." Jamie looked at Evan.

"He's lying. My name is Evan McGregor. I come from wealth. My family is next to royalty in California. I have never hurt a child in my life! Now let me loose!" Evan pulled furiously at his restraints, waved his arms, and kicked his feet so violently he lost one of his shoes. Kate walked over and picked it up. She turned it over and showed Jamie. It was an Italian-made Botticelli shoe, with the same tread pattern found at the crime scene in Saline.

Aaron walked over to Jamie and handed him the photo of his son. Jamie took it.

"That's my little boy," Aaron said.

Jamie looked at first the front photo, then the back. He did not hand it to Kate, and she didn't ask to see it. Jamie turned to Evan. He told him he was under arrest. He explained that the shoe-print evidence found at the crime scene in Saline matched the shoes he was wearing and the fact that DNA obtained from the photos would surely match his.

Evan stared at him in disbelief. "That's your case? Are you kidding me? Evidence obtained at the home of a serial murderer. OK, you got me. Now get me out of this contraption and put the cuffs on me, please. There is not a prosecutor in the state of Michigan who could win that case. My lawyer will have me out of this shitty state by noon!"

Jamie bristled at Evan's response. Evan sat smiling smugly as he watched the realization of what he had just said sink in to Jamie's countenance.

"There is another way," Kate said quietly. All three men looked at her like she had just stepped off a flying saucer with two round-eyed alien companions. "We could go back to your house, Jamie. Crack open a couple beers . . . play some cards . . . see what develops . . ."

Evan looked at her, mouth open like she'd lost her mind. Then he looked at Jamie. He did not like what he saw. Jamie looked like he'd just discovered the final word of a crossword puzzle he'd been working on for some time. Jamie's features softened. He turned to Aaron. "Can this Gatekeeper business end tonight? Will you let me handle justice from now on?"

Kate was already climbing the ladder. Evan, still unable to close his mouth, listened as Jamie and Aaron continued their conversation. "I don't want to see this man ever again. I don't want to find his body propped up somewhere for the public to see. I want to climb up that ladder and know the world is a safer place to live. Is that possible?" Jamie asked Aaron.

"There is nothing I would like more!" Aaron said. "I've been toying with the idea of filling this old dungeon in, anyway. It would make a good resting place for Mr. McGregor. That way, I could park my old hot rod on his grave!" Aaron spat on the floor at Evan's feet. Evan closed his mouth in response and swallowed hard. Jamie walked over and put one foot on the ladder. He looked back at Aaron. "*For justice?*" he said.

"*For justice,*" Aaron echoed.

As Jamie climbed the ladder, Aaron walked over, made a few adjustments to the camera, and hit play. As the plywood hatch dropped back into place, he picked up the knife and faced Evan. Evan McGregor, you have committed a crime against an innocent child, and Justice cries out from the grave. We must answer. Suddenly Evan found his voice and began to scream!

The young boy beamed with excitement as he put the manila envelopes up on the counter. "I'd like to mail these," he said to the postmaster. "How much?" he asked.

The postmaster weighed one of the packages. "That will be eighty cents apiece, and it looks like you have thirty-five." He tapped away at the calculator for a few seconds. "Looks like your total will be $28."

The boy took the crisp hundred-dollar bill the man with the bright blue eyes had given him and laid it on the counter. After receiving his change, he bolted for the door, mission accomplished. The postmaster picked up the padded manila envelopes and examined them. They each had a different destination, return address was the same, *For Justice!*

Edwards Brothers Malloy
Thorofare, NJ USA
September 10, 2012